Perfect
Imperfection

Also by John Staples

White Lies and Other Deceptions
Make Love, Drive Freeway, Now and Then

PERFECT IMPERFECTION

JOHN STAPLES

Published by Alabaster Book Publishing
North Carolina

Perfect Imperfection is a work of fiction. Any references to real people, events, establishments, organizations or locales are intended only to give the fiction a sense of reality and authenticity. Other names, characters, places and incidents portrayed herein are either the product of the author's imagination or are used fictionally.

PERFECT IMPERFECTION Copyright 2008 by John Staples. All rights reserved. Printed in the United States of America. No part of this book may be reproduced or reused in any manner whatsoever without written permission except in the case of brief quotations embodied in critical articles and reviews.

Published by Alabaster Publishing Company
P.O. Box 401
Kernersville, North Carolina 27285
Visit our web site at: Http://www.publishingalabaster.com

Book cover design by John Staples
Book design by David Shaffer

FIRST EDITION

ISBN 13: 978-0-9815763-8-1
ISBN 10: 0-9815763-8-9

Library of Congress Control Number: 2008943881

Dedication

To my wife, Jane, and our children, John and Kara, who have brought untold hours of joy and comfort to me.

Acknowledgements

I owe the value of this book, whatever it may be, to many friends, relatives and associates I have known through the years and who have stood by me in good times and bad. They have been my eyes and ears on many occasions and have been my best supporters and often my most trusted critics.

Special thanks go to members of the Triad Writers Group who helped keep me on track when I suffered the pangs of writer's block or failed to see the obvious literary flaws that crop up from time to time. Their patience, concern and critical viewpoints have been a constant element of encouragement and support. All are published authors whose works I have read and admired. They are:

Joanne Clarey: *Twisted Truth* and The *Hummingbird Falls* series.
Kathryn Fisher: *Up a Tree with Tatie Wee*
Helen Goodman: *Jess, Murder in Eden, The Blue Goose is Dead, Toxic Waste* and others.
Lynette Hall Hampton: The Willow Hinshaw Series, *Duo of Opposites, Writer to Writer* and others.
D.E. Joyner: *Mistaken Identity* and *Who Killed Zaida Moore.*
Dixie Land: *Serenity, Return to Serenity, Promises to Keep, Circle of Secrets, Exit Wounds* and *Finding Faith.*
David Shaffer: The Harry Caine mystery series including *Paid in Full, Dead Right, Wake Up Call* and *Burned.*

I am also indebted to Larry Jakubsen for his incisive critiques laced with wit and good humor and for his promising soon-to-be published nostalgic sports reverie, *The Courthouse Tigers*. Many thanks also to Chuck Smithers for his good-natured comments and critiques.

Finally, my special thanks go to all the people in my hometown of Kernersville, North Carolina whose characters and conflicts have filled my life with wonder and awe and have made it rich and rewarding beyond comparison. They are the heart and soul of Perfect Imperfection.

Other works by John Staples:
White Lies and Other Deceptions, Harlan Publishing Co. 2002.
Make Love, Drive Freeway Every Now and Zen, Alabaster Publishing, 2005.

"Apparently, the varieties of imperfection in the world constitute the perfection that God intended, for that is what She got."
Cee Edmunds

Chapter 1

Outside it was cool, foggy and damp. Jesse Stallings looked at his watch. Four a.m., no time for a rational man to be up and about.

Nonetheless, Jesse couldn't sleep. In fact, he seldom slept more than four hours at a stretch. His nasal passages closed and he had trouble breathing. The female ear, nose and throat specialist said he had a deviated septum. She said he could either use some nasal spray for the rest of his life or have the septum straightened. She could fix it for only a thousand dollars or so. He opted for the nasal spray.

That was five years ago. Now he was up again before daybreak. He went to the bathroom, turned on the hot water faucet, let it run for a minute or so and then filled a plastic cup with the hot liquid. He held it up to his nose and breathed in the warm, humid air. In a minute he could breathe through both nostrils again. He poured out the water, washed the cup and then placed it back on the counter to be ready for the next day.

Looking into the mirror, Jesse studied the ruddy skin of his face for a moment, then the thinning hair on his head. The folds under his eyes were beginning to sag a little. For the first time, he felt his age—the down side of fifty. It showed. He splashed a little cold water on his face and put aside the thought that he had lived more than half a century. He decided a little breakfast, even at this hour, would do him good. He went to the kitchen, poured himself a bowl of bran flakes and sprinkled them with artificial sweetener. He put half a cup of milk over the cereal, sat down and tuned the TV to CNN to watch the morning news. There were rumblings in the Mideast, the home mortgage industry was beginning to experience signs of a melt-down, as was the ice in the polar caps. A few more years and all hell might break loose. Thus far, it was a fairly normal day.

Thirty minutes later Stallings was still wandering around the house searching for something to do. He knew he could not go back to sleep and that sleep would not come despite his longing for it. He would be awake for at least another two hours before becoming drowsy again. By then it would be time to get dressed, read the morning paper and prepare for another day at the Conners Hill News.

Also by then his wife Janice would be awake, as well as their two children. Everyone would be getting ready for the day's routine. Janice would be going off to school to teach reading to her third-graders. Jon and Cara would be leaving for their day of classes as well.

Perfect Imperfection

Jesse, dressed in a dark blue terrycloth bathrobe and slippers, opened the door from the kitchen to the carport and walked outside into the cool, damp air. It was still dark, but from the glow of the fog enshrouded streetlight at the end of the driveway, he could see the newspaper lying just on the edge of his front yard. He was about to head for the paper when he noticed a car moving slowly up the hill into the subdivision. The car's headlights were out, but the outline of the vehicle was distinct, as it was bathed in the back light of the neighborhood swimming pool complex just below the crest of the hill.

Jesse couldn't tell much about the car except the shape, like that of a large black, four-door, European-style sedan—perhaps an Audi or a Mercedes. It crept slowly toward the top of the hill. Jesse stayed in the shadows of the carport to avoid being noticed. He tried to see who was in the car as it passed by, but the light was not bright enough and the car's windows were heavily tinted. He watched the vehicle move slowly down the street and come to a quiet stop in front of Ernie Blaine's house. The back door of the vehicle opened and a woman emerged. She nearly stumbled, then grabbed the car door to regain her balance as she tilted backwards. A hand emerged from the door holding a dark fur-trimmed coat and something that appeared light and flimsy.

Vivian Blaine laughed as she jerked the coat and the lacy undergarment from the hand and let the latter fall to the ground. She bent over, picked it up and waved unsteadily to whoever was in the back seat of the car. She touched her fingers to her lips, blew a kiss to the dark interior and started toward the door of the modest brick bungalow. The car door closed and the vehicle picked up speed and was soon out of sight.

Stallings glanced at his watch: 5:45 a.m. He continued to watch as Vivian, an attractive blonde in her early thirties, fumbled in her pocketbook for her door key. When she found it, she dropped it, picked it up and dropped it again. She picked it up once more, haltingly inserted the key into the lock and opened the door. A light came on in the Blaine foyer as she stepped inside to face her husband.

Chapter 2

Stallings could not hear the voices from inside the Blaine house three doors down the street, but if he had heard them, he would have winced at the conversation:

"Where the hell have you been this time, Viv?" Ernie Blaine shouted. "Do you have no respect for yourself or your family? How long do you expect me to put up with this? I can tell you it won't be much longer. I'm sick to death of your drinking and cavorting with God knows who or what, and I won't take it forever. I'll get a lawyer and kick your ass out of this house in a heartbeat. Just keep it up and I'll show you. I'll put you out on the street where you belong! So long and Sayonara, baby. Good-bye and good riddance, that's what it'll be."

Her senses dulled from alcohol, Vivian Blaine would not put up a fight. She would only wave her hand, smile stupidly and act as if she had just returned from lunch with a friend. She brushed past her husband of ten years and headed for the bathroom down the hall. Once inside, she locked the door and sprawled out on the floor, her head tilted toward the open toilet bowl. "Jesus Christ," she said to herself, "he never closes the freakin' lid. Why are men so goddamned stupid?" She wanted to throw up, but she could only gag.

She could barely hear her husband's plaintive voice outside the door. "Viv, please listen to me. Think of the children. Think of your mother and father. Think what the neighbors will think seeing you wander in here at five-thirty in the morning. For God's sake, Viv, think of what you're doing to yourself and to the rest of the family."

"Go away, Ernie. I'm tired of freaking thinking. What the hell has thinking ever gotten you? You've got a job you hate, a boss who thinks you're a sniveling suck-up and a wife who's had more fun in one night than in ten years of being married to you. Think about that for a while and leave me alone. I'll be here with your supper ready when you get home tonight. What more do you think you deserve?"

"Okay, Viv, I'm getting the kids up and ready for school, but I'm not forgetting this. It's gone on way too long. I'm telling you now that I'm not going to take it any more. I mean it, I'm not. I'd rather rot in hell than see you burn yourself up with all this boozing and carousing. I'd rather kill you than see you do it to yourself. You hear me? I've reached the breaking point. I won't stand for it any more."

After a decade of marriage, Vivian Blaine knew her husband better than he knew himself. She thought he had neither the courage nor the dignity to do what needed to be done: to beat her or cut her loose. If he'd done either, she would have respected him a little—not enough perhaps, but a little. If he had kept his word and thrown her out, she would have tried to be a better wife, a better woman even. She would have known he cared enough about her to fight with her, to lash out with more than empty words. She wanted a man who could give her up or give up his own life because he loved her. She had become convinced that Ernest Blaine was incapable of loving anyone enough to let go of his fears.

CHAPTER 3

In another part of town Dave Devlin, a private investigator, was getting ready for bed. He'd been out on a stakeout in an affluent Conners Hill neighborhood. He hadn't intended to conduct an all-night surveillance but merely to follow a policeman whose wife suspected him of some extra-curricular affair.

Devlin was an affable Irishman whose face was a picture of contentment. It was a pleasant face painted with blue-green eyes and warm pink skin slightly mottled with reddish freckles. He had an elfish grin that made him look as if he'd had one mug too many. The stakeout hadn't been planned; it just happened, one thing leading to another until something turned up.

When Devlin left home that night, he'd told his wife Mary he expected to be back by midnight because his assignment was a pretty routine affair. The officer he was hired to watch was suspected by his wife of having a fling with a local barmaid. Devlin knew the officer and suspected the affair was nothing more than a harmless flirtation. But he also knew that flirtations sometimes run amok, and who was he to turn down a hundred bucks—his standard fee—for a few hours surveillance?

The PI had anticipated simply following the officer to a local sports bar to wait and see if he and the barmaid left the place together or separately, and, if separately, to see if they joined up later at her apartment. Once at the tavern, Devlin decided to make the assignment as pleasant as possible. He entered the bar, drank a beer or two, and watched an early season football game on TV. He chatted casually with both the cop and the barmaid while observing their interaction first hand. A believer in the art of hiding in plain sight, Devlin knew that if he was enjoying himself, he would not be suspected of spying on anyone.

About 9 p.m., the phone in the tavern rang. Sissy Spangler, the barmaid, recognized the voice at the other end of the line.

"Is Alan there, Sissy?" Anne Malloy said in an icy tone.

"Who wants to know?" Spangler replied.

"It's Anne, you itchy bitch. You know, Anne Malloy, your boyfriend's wife."

"Oh, Anal Annie. Why didn't you say so? Hold on, I'll take my tongue out of his ear so he can hear you."

Sissy held the phone at arm's length and shouted across the crowded room. "Hey, Alan, Annie's on the phone. She wants to know if you can come home and give her a little pickle tickle so she can remember what it's like."

"I don't want to talk to her," said Sgt. Alan Malloy. "She's the only woman I know who can smell your breath over the telephone."

"Hell, Alan, most of us can smell your breath over the telephone. It's the one that smells like wet fur. Seriously, Alan, Annie says it's urgent. Something about Chief Grady needing you ASAP."

"Oh, all right. Hand me the freakin' phone."

Malloy held the receiver about a foot away from his ear as he listened to his wife give him hell about where he was and what he was doing with Sissy, the "Cocker Spangler bitch." Nonetheless, he got the message that Stanfield Grady, Conners Hill's police chief, wanted him down at the station right away.

Devlin waited for Malloy to leave the bar and gave him a few minutes head start before leaving himself. As far as the PI was concerned, his work for the night was over. However, he was curious as to what kind of assignment the local police were conducting on such short notice. He decided to satisfy his curiosity by finding out where Malloy was going. He drove downtown, pulled into a back parking lot behind the row of offices on South Main Street adjacent to the Conners Hill Police Department's basement entrance. He parked behind a large hedgerow separating the businesses from the police lot and waited patiently for Malloy for nearly half an hour. He passed the time by listening to a CD of some big band music featuring the great old-time drummer Gene Krupa. Soon Malloy and three other officers came out, got into an unmarked car and pulled out of the station area. All four were dressed in coats and ties.

Perfect Imperfection

Devlin let the officers pull out onto South Main and get about a quarter of a mile away before taking off after them in his black Camaro. His curiosity heightened when they turned onto Old Winston Road, drove half a mile or so to a subdivision known as Bramblewood. They went a couple of blocks past the subdivision's community swimming pool to a house on a cul-de-sac at the end of Willowgate Lane. Finally the car pulled into the drive of a home that lay about forty yards off the road, totally surrounded by woods. Devlin cut his lights, drove past the residence, and started to stop. He noticed a small trail just big enough to shield a car from oncoming headlights and just across from the large house's entrance. He figured if he backed into it just far enough, he could see nearly all the way up the driveway and still be pretty well hidden from view.

Devlin took note of a number of cars already parked in the driveway of the large, two-story colonial-style house. From his vantage point he could see other cars on their way to the residence. One, a large black limousine with a Virginia license plate, eased into the drive, and six young women emerged from the stretch limo's back door and headed toward the house. Most of them were fashionably dressed in dark pant suits or tightly-clinging black dresses. Joking and laughing as they got out of the car, several carried half-empty cocktail glasses. One, a blonde, moved with the grace of a thoroughbred mare. If she had been drinking with the others, it wasn't apparent.

Devlin was intrigued. What kind of assignment brought four plain-clothed policemen and a bevy of attractive women to a late-evening get-together in one of the town's most upscale neighborhoods? When another large sedan pulled into the drive and four men dressed in evening clothes got out and headed for the house, it dawned on him. He recognized one of the men from the days he had spent giving testimony in divorce cases in the Falwell County Courthouse in Selwin. There was no mistaking the man nor his limp. He was a somewhat rotund, balding but square-jawed chief of the county's Superior Court, Judge Phillip J. Feldman, better known to local lawyers as "Felonious Phil." A man Devlin could not identify met the four men at the front door of the home and ushered them inside with firm handshakes. Politics, thought Devlin.

Though he was tired and bored, the P.I. stayed in his car for the better part of three hours. He wanted to see who left the party with whom and who, if anyone, stayed behind. He was not surprised when Feldman and the three men with him emerged from the house only an hour or so after they arrived. He was surprised when four others, including Malloy and another local cop, left the house with the attractive blonde around 2 a.m. All four got into the back seat of the black limousine before it drove away. A few minutes later, two more men came out of the house, got into the unmarked police car and left the premises.

Devlin wanted to follow the limousine with Malloy. However, as the gathering appeared to be breaking up, he was afraid he might be spotted by someone. Once the coast was clear, he pulled out of the woods and headed to Suzie's Diner, an all-night eatery not far from downtown Conners Hill. He decided to have a breakfast doughnut and a cup of coffee before going home and going to bed. On his way into the restaurant, he stopped at a newspaper rack outside the front door to pick up a copy of the Selwin Daily Mirror, the county daily.

Unexpectedly, the two plain-clothes policemen who had driven away from the Bramblegate party in the unmarked car were in the diner when he arrived. As soon as he saw them he started to turn around and leave but decided otherwise. He did what he most always did when he felt surprised or out of place. He straightened his back and pretended there was nothing to worry about. As far as he knew, neither of the cops knew him. If they did, they didn't show it. He was sure he was in the clear when he took a booth just behind them and they began to talk of their assignment that night. By the time they were done, Devlin knew that Sissy Spangler was the least of Anne Malloy's problems.

Chapter 4

What he had seen early that morning was still on Jesse Stallings' mind when he arrived for work at the Conners Hill News around 8:30 a.m. He knew Ernie Blaine, a former claims adjuster turned automobile salesman. He saw him often at church and considered him a good and decent fellow. He knew Vivian Blaine only by reputation. She seldom went to church and did not participate in many formal civic activities. He had heard that, in addition to her stunning good looks, she was a better than average secretary, a decent housekeeper and a devoted mother. He heard rumors also that she sometimes drank too much, talked too candidly about her past, and treated her husband as if he were a temporary inconvenience. He also heard she had a weakness for attractive men with money and power and that they more often than not responded with the kind of attention she sought.

As was his usual routine on weekday mornings, Jesse stopped by the coffee urn in the front lobby of the Conners Hill News. He filled a Styrofoam cup with the hot liquid and carefully laced it with a packet of artificial sweetener and a dash of non-dairy creamer. After taking a sip or two, he strolled over to the front desk, nodded to the new receptionist who was talking on the telephone and picked up his mail from a circular file on a small mahogany table just outside the business office.

He poked his head into the office and spoke to Becky Martin, the News' bookkeeper and office manager. He liked her cheerfulness and graceful acceptance of others, not to mention her organizational skills. Her tact and diplomacy made her a force to be reckoned with. She spoke her mind but always with a warm smile that tended to put one at ease. Besides, she was a good listener and a ready audience for Jesse's tall tales.

"Say, Becky, did you hear what happened in the parking lot behind Conners Hill High School last night?" Stallings asked.

"No, but I'm sure you're going to tell me," said Martin.

"Well, it seems one of our local cops was passing by the school around midnight when he noticed a car with its lights on way back in the corner of the lot near the Fourth of July Park. He drove around to the rear of the building over toward the park and when he got close enough to see inside the car, he found a guy in the front seat reading a magazine and a girl in the back seat polishing her fingernails. He pulled up beside the couple, got out, knocked on the driver's side window and asked the driver what he and the girl were doing in the parking lot at that time of night."

"'Sir, as you can see, I'm reading and she's fixing her nails,' the young driver said. Somewhat perplexed, the policeman looked at the young man, then glanced in the back seat at the girl. Scratching his head, he asked: 'How old are you young folks?'

"'Well, officer,' said the driver, 'I'm twenty-one, but in ten minutes she'll be eighteen.'"

Becky laughed. "Get out of here, Jesse. I thought you were serious. You and I both know that didn't happen."

"Well, it could, couldn't it?" Jesse said as he slipped out the door and began to climb the L-shaped flight of stairs leading to the newsroom. Walking up the stairs, he thought *Why should I be serious? Life is fatal but not serious.*

Arriving at the second floor cubicle he called an office, Stallings hurriedly thumbed through the stack of mail he had just picked up. He looked to see if he had received anything from Wolf Johnson, Conners Hill's town attorney. Johnson, a fastidious dresser with a penchant for colorful suits and expensive shoes, was one of the News' biggest critics as well as one of its most consistent readers. He felt that if a town was big enough to have a newspaper, it was big enough to have a newspaper with high editorial standards, one that did not pander too much to advertisers nor hire inexperienced or unqualified reporters. "If you're going to do it, then do it right," he often said to Jesse following his discovery of an offensive gaff in a story.

Stallings' retort was almost always the same: "If you're gonna complain, Wolf, then complain to the guy who owns the paper and hires the help and tries to look good in the process. Sometimes looking good to him means having a big desk, a big car, a big house and a big bank account. Occasionally that translates into being a big pain in the ass. But, like the rest of us, publishers are a mixed bag. They want to do good, but they know you have to do well to do good. You can't keep good reporters and editors without paying them a living wage. And you can't pay good wages without making good money." Jesse sometimes thought the Conners Hill News' publisher was more interested in doing well than doing good. No doubt most newspaper editors had the same thought..

What Stallings was searching for in the mail was a note from Johnson regarding a pending suit filed by a disgruntled homeowner over a dog caught running loose in the neighborhood. The angry homeowner turned the dog over to the county's animal control officer. The owner contended the pet, a mix of Collie and German Shepherd, was not running loose but had been stolen. The neighbor said the dog was dangerous and should be put to sleep. He said the dog barked all night and kept him awake. The News' publisher, Owen Jobs, was the dog's owner. He filed a suit against the town on grounds of unlawful confiscation of private property. Wolf Johnson was trying to find a way to satisfy both parties without going to trial.

There was no note among the twenty or thirty pieces of mail Stallings had collected at the front desk. Perhaps Johnson had worked something out with Jobs in private. Jesse hoped so. After all, the town did not steal the dog. A policeman picked it up in the street near the caller's house, and although it had a rabies immunization tag and the name of the owner on the collar, it was running loose when the police arrived.

While looking for the non-existent note from Johnson, Jesse could not let go of the thought of where Ernest Blaine's wife had been or who she was with that morning. Nor could he dismiss the thought that Ernie was a hard-working, decent man who provided an adequate living for his family, gave time to his church, to the local Rotarians and to projects of the Conners Hill Chamber of Commerce. He wondered what would drive the wife of such a man to risk losing her husband, her children and her reputation for a night of extramarital sex or whatever it was that sent her out into the world looking for a temporary solution to stress, boredom or frustration? He believed it must be something more than the need to feel desirable to someone other than her husband.

Chapter 5

Stallings strolled past half a dozen cubicles on his way to his desk. In the middle aisle he picked up a copy of the Mirror, the county's only daily newspaper. He sat down to finish his coffee, glance at the paper's headlines and then thumb through the news releases and other assorted pieces of mail on his desk.

It was only 8:30 and he had twenty minutes to sift through the mail before heading up Main Street to sit in on the week's district court session. Finding no note from Johnson, he searched the mail for the day's court docket. He smiled when he found it and saw that the presiding judge would be A. L. Sherf, one of the county's most flamboyant decision-makers.

Though rigorously conscientious, Sherf was always good for a laugh and more often than not for a decision that was both riveting and thought-provoking. Despite the depth of Sherf's perception and logical reasoning, Jesse felt it was unlikely the somewhat eccentric barrister would ever climb the ladder of the state's judicial hierarchy. Simply put, he was too independent and too politically incorrect. Besides, he was a Republican in a state whose legal ranks were filled mostly with died-in-the-wool Democrats, good ol' boys who knew not to be too controversial or to make too many waves lest they disturb the God-given order they had inherited from their Civil War ancestors. "Once you start rocking the boat, it don't stop 'til you've been thrown out," a wizened old Superior Court judge once told him, adding that a "balanced view and a cool head" were more important than "a quick decision and a heavy hand." Sherf took the advice seriously but not seriously enough to prevent him from relying on his own instincts when circumstances called for it, which was more often than the state's judicial establishment thought necessary.

To Stallings, it was a pleasure to watch Abraham Lincoln "Linc" Sherf operate, particularly if one were not the one on the operating table. Then it was like going under the knife without anesthesia, the treatment being worse than the disease.

Stallings checked his watch and decided to head to the town hall courtroom. Once there he seated himself in the third row behind the prosecutor's table. As the bailiff began the day's proceedings with a "Hear ye, hear ye, everyone please rise," Judge Sherf entered the courtroom at a swift pace, his square jaw jutted forward, his thick locks of dark brown hair falling over his forehead, the folds of his black robe flowing majestically in his wake.

Perfect Imperfection

As soon as the judge had taken his seat, he waved a finger toward the waiting bailiff, who cried out again: "Hear ye, hear ye, the District Court of Falwell County, the great state of North Carolina, United States of America, is now in session. Please be seated."

The ritual was an archaic but effective means of announcing that court was about to begin and an indication that the proceeding was a solemn one. The formality took some of the mundane monotony out of a never-ending lineup of routine traffic charges, pretrial hearings and assorted misdemeanor cases.. Often the district court docket was more interesting than the proceedings themselves, especially when it contained unexpected names similar to those of influential local citizens such as a miscreant minister or a philandering marriage counselor.

On at least one occasion Judge Sherf let his elfish wit run rampant. He might have thrown the entire courtroom into a circus atmosphere had it not been for his inherently imposing demeanor. Such was the case when, during the calling of several routine traffic cases, a young black defendant nattily dressed in a white shirt, sport coat and bright red tie rose to defend himself against the charge of running a stop sign.

As the assistant district attorney handling the morning's files called out the defendant's name and asked how he pleaded, the young man rose and said to the judge: "Awh plead nawt guilty, me Lawd."

Judge Sherf lowered his reading glasses and peered upward over their silver rims and away from the papers he was arranging. He looked quizzically at the young man, who innocently returned his glare, eyeball-to-eyeball.

"I beg your pardon," said Judge Sherf, "but would you please repeat that."

"Awh plead nawt guilty, me Lawd," the young man chimed once again, his thick British accent eliciting smiles throughout the courtroom.

"I thought that's what you said," said Sherf, turning his head to speak to the prosecutor. "Mr. Keifer, what is this man charged with?"

"He ran a stop sign at the corner of West Fontaine and Stafford Road," said the prosecutor.

"Where are you from, young man?" Sherf asked the defendant.

"Jamaica, me Lawd."

"Do you understand the traffic laws of the United States and of the state of North Carolina?"

"Awh hahve studied them rahthuh intensely, me Lawd."

"And do you understand that when you see a red stop sign at a street corner, it means that you should come to a full stop before proceeding through the intersection?"

"Awh do, me Lawd."

"And why did you not stop on the occasion in question?"

"Well, me Lawd, 'twas laike this: Oye'm a graduate student at West Fontaine University and Oye was late for me clahss in American history, and as Oye approached the intersection, Oye looked both ways and saw nawthing coming. Oye decided 'twahs more prudent to maike it to me clahss on time than to stop for a bloomin' sawgn."

Sherf turned his head to the arresting officer sitting at the table with the solicitor. "Officer, did you see any other cars entering the intersection at the time this defendant says he ran the stop sign?"

"No, I didn't, your honor."

Sherf thanked the officer for doing his duty in bringing in the defendant and for his candor concerning the circumstances of the traffic citation. Then he turned to the defendant. "Well, then, it's like this," he said, banging his gavel on the wooden block on the bar. "Any young man who has the good sense to call me My Lord can't be all bad. Case dismissed."

In the next case Judge Sherf ordered a young East Falwell High School student to pick up trash on the school campus every afternoon for a month. He had thrown an empty cigarette pack out the window of his car as he was leaving the campus one day.

Sherf often launched into a stern lecture about the seriousness of disobeying the law, particularly laws that were designed to improve the looks and condition of the environment. As he was fond of making the punishment fit the crime, he often came up with ways to have environmental offenders serve their communities rather than charging them fines or sending them to jail.

Chapter 6

Stallings looked forward to each week's court session not only because it gave him a chance to sit and listen to Judge Sherf, but also because it gave him a chance to get away from the constant ringing of the phone on his desk. Nothing jangled his nerves more than a telephone that rang every ten minutes or so. He looked forward as well to the few minutes he would spend in the office of Irma Robrock, the no-nonsense magistrate whose speech and demeanor were as refreshing as Judge Sherf's. On one occasion he got more than he bargained for.

Robrock's office was just off a narrow hallway that led from the rear of the upstairs district courtroom to a fire escape at the back of the second floor hallway. Reporters often stopped in at the magistrate's office before court to listen to the conversations between her and the day's presiding judge, or between her and the arresting officers and the assistant district attorneys.

During his trip to the court the previous week, Robrock launched into a tirade about what she considered the excessive paperwork she was required to do in preparation for the cases she was to hear and decide. "It's just damned foolishness to make six copies of a motion to dismiss a simple civil proceeding," she was saying as Jesse entered her office.

"Don't get your grits in a knot," said Dan Davis, an assistant D.A. "You know how nasty the state gets if you don't make multiple records of all court proceedings. It makes no difference whether it's from a magistrate or a Superior Court judge, it's all the same: Scrimp on the copies and pretty soon half the court system won't know what the other half is doing."

"Poppycock," said Robrock. "One half the system doesn't know what the other half is doing now, but at least somebody's getting six copies of what they don't know."

Stallings decided the discussion was not one he wished to join, although one of his pet peeves was redundant paperwork. He greeted Robrock briefly, then took his leave to find a seat as close to the front of the courtroom as possible. He wanted to be able to hear both the on-and-off-the-record comments of the judge, who again happened to be Abraham Lincoln Sherf.

The upstairs courtroom was located just above the fire station in downtown Conners Hill. It was a relatively small chamber, with only about seven rows of seats on each side of a middle aisle. There were perhaps six seats per row on each side of the aisle.

After Jesse had eased into a seat behind the prosecutor's table, he got out his notebook and pen and began to look over the day's docket. It contained nothing more than the names of the defendants, the dates of their arrests, the charges against them and whether or not the cases were civil or criminal ones. He saw nothing much that looked interesting except for a preliminary hearing for two youths who had torn a hole through the wall of a downtown business establishment and had been caught by local police as they attempted to squeeze a 27-inch television set through an 18-inch hole. Both were apprehended as they tried to figure out how to get the TV through the hole.

In the meantime Judge Sherf began reviewing the day's traffic violations. He had disposed of three or four cases when the sound of a gunshot rang out from the back of the courtroom. Instantly, an agonizing cry came from the hallway leading past the magistrate's office. "Oh, my God, oh, my God. I've been shot, I've been shot," cried Sgt. D.G. Makepeace.

The court bailiff and several policemen and sheriff's deputies in the courtroom headed immediately for the door that led to the back hall. Others in the room waiting for their cases to be tried began to get up to leave. Judge Sherf banged his gavel down two or three times. "Keep your seats, ladies and gentlemen. Let the officers here handle the situation. Do not get out of your seats. The officers will take care of whatever needs to be done."

Jesse's first instinct was to get up and see what had happened. He would have done so had he not known that Sherf's words were meant for everyone in the room, including the press.

Within minutes, a couple of firemen and emergency medical technicians from the station below entered the court chambers, bringing with them emergency medical kits and a stretcher. After entering the back hall and working with the wounded deputy sheriff for several minutes, the firemen carried him out the door on the stretcher. The sheet covering him was soaked with blood. It was evident from the look on his face and from his anguished moan that he was in great pain. In another minute or two, an emergency vehicle pulled out of the station bay, its siren wailing, its medical technicians hunched over the limp and near lifeless body of the wounded deputy. The ambulance headed for the county hospital in Selwin, twelve miles away.

Judge Sherf called a brief recess in the court proceedings and headed back to the magistrate's office to find out what had happened. As he approached the door to the hallway, he noticed that the bullet that had pierced the wounded man's torso had also gone through the door behind the deputy. It left a splintered hole in the door. In a few minutes, other deputies began searching the room for the bullet. They found it lodged in the heel of a shoe worn by a man sitting a couple of rows behind the solicitor's table. It had passed within a foot of where Jesse was seated.

Judge Sherf returned to the courtroom and announced that the day's court session would be postponed until a later date. "I apologize for the inconvenience, but under the circumstances, I believe we need to get to the bottom of what has occurred here this morning," he said. He told the solicitor to notify the county clerk of the session's postponement and make plans to notify the defendants' lawyers and witnesses when it would be rescheduled.

Stallings left the courtroom with the others. He returned a couple of hours later to see Irma Robrock and find out exactly what had happened.

"You won't believe it, Jesse, but one of our dumb-ass deputies was twirling his revolver around his finger like some western movie cowboy when it went off. The bullet tore a hole through Sergeant Makepeace. I called the hospital just a few minutes ago. D.G. is in the operating room as we speak. The .38-caliber slug went through his stomach and out his back. There's some serious doubt as to whether or not he'll survive."

Jesse left the magistrate's office and headed straight back to the Conners Hill News building to write the story of what had happened. Makepeace was a friend and a good law enforcement officer. He had once informed Jesse about Mabel Rogers, the head of a notorious prostitution ring who owned a house in an affluent section of Conners Hill. A follow-up of Jesse's story about the house and its so-called "hostess" had made the front page of the county's daily newspaper. He wished Makepeace well.

Chapter 7

Vivian Tyler Blaine's husband Ernie had been a Marine Corps officer, a high school teacher and a law student at the University of North Carolina before doing a stint as a claims adjuster for one of the nation's largest automobile insurance companies. Vivian was a senior at Grandboro College when she met him. She had been introduced to him by his aunt, Sadie Fontaine, the widow of R.A. Fontaine, a wealthy tobacco farmer, warehouse owner and merchant who lived in Fontaine, a small town not far from Greenville, North Carolina, where Vivian had grown up. Sadie Fontaine had moved back to Conners Hill after the death of her husband and into an apartment adjoining the home of her older sister Carrie Whiteacre, Ernie's maternal grandmother.

Vivian's father, William Harrington Beeler, was an intelligent and prosperous businessman who had graduated among the top of his class at N.C. State University and then obtained a master's degree from Trinity College before it became better known as Duke University. He had become wealthy by selling tobacco harvesting equipment to plantation owners down East. Her mother, a strikingly beautiful débutante better known for her vivacious personality than her occasional moodiness, had been among the most popular girls at Grandboro College, a church-affiliated all-girls school in Grandboro..

Vivian was the oldest of the Beelers' three children. Like her mother, she was attractive, bright and outgoing. Also like her mother, she was subject to sudden, unpredictable mood swings that could turn her from a flowering beauty to a sulking introvert. In the eight weeks he dated her before proposing marriage, Ernie had seen only her alluring beauty and her vivacious personality. Vivian, he thought, was a perfect name for a woman of such vitality and charm. It was not until his first visit to the Beeler home in Greenville that Ernie began to get a glimpse of the life that would later haunt both him and his soon-to-be bride.

Chapter 8

As far as Ernie Blaine could remember, he had been in love all his life. No doubt his love had been fostered in the bosom of his mother, whose coal-black hair and broad smile had remained with him throughout his life. It was not until several years after he had finished college, done his stint in the Marine Corps, returned to Conners Hill and taken a job as an instructor at a local military academy that he became aware of just how strong his attraction to his mother was.

It was about the time that he met Baccara Thomason, a tall, elegant brunette with a slender, lithe figure, pouting lips and a cleft chin. She was a blind date for a St. Patrick's Day outing at a Grandboro supper club called Green's. When he picked her up at the state college for women in Grandboro, she was wearing a dark green corduroy dress with a full skirt, "penny loafers" and a smile that melted into sadness and back at the slightest glance. On that first date Ernie found her an awkward dancer whose exaggerated hip movements were out of sync with the late rock and roll of the early 1960s, but when the music was slow and he put his arms around her and she held onto him as if he was the only man alive, he felt that he was the only one who had ever held her close and felt the soft touch of her small, full breasts against his chest. The first time she kissed him it was with an open mouth and lips so pliable they melted into his own. From that moment on he was destined to wallow in what he thought was love and to love what he thought he had to have to be satisfied with life.

Six years later he woke up in a cold sweat in a small dormitory room in Blairsville, Pennsylvania and recalled his dream of seeing the visitors' book at a funeral and know that Baccara Thomason had died of Hodgkin's disease at that very moment in a Texas hospital. He would finish his work at the insurance company's auto repair school in Blairsville three days later and return home to North Carolina. His mother greeted him at the front door with the words, "Son, I'm sorry to have to give you some bad news, but Baccara Thomason has died."

"I know," said Ernie. "I was there."

He was not there, but his mind was.

It was perhaps the saddest day of his life until the death of his mother, but it was an event that later relieved him of the strain of guilt for having left the brave but naive woman-child to escape his own jealousy and self-torture. She was dead and he could get on with his life and give all his mind's attention to his wife, Vivian, whom he had married to escape the torment of loving Baccara and never knowing whether he was loved by her or was merely an instrument of her attempt to escape from what she believed was a less than well-to-do family. Despite her insecurities, Baccara had an uncle who was a physician and a cousin who was a highly respected newspaper columnist with a flair for making readers laugh and cry and think.

Aside from being what Ernie thought was the most beautiful woman he had ever seen, Baccara was a woman of no small intellect. She had achieved remarkable grades at the largest university for women in the state and had a flair for poetry and words whose depth sometimes exceeded her ability to comprehend the profound despair that showed through them. She could write as clearly as the smooth white skin of her impeccable face. It was a smoothness more like the cream from a fresh bottle of milk than human skin. Her words, though seemingly childlike, were clear and lucid as glass but also sweet and sorrowful and as full of a hopeless longing to know who she was and where she was going as his own.

Ernie and Baccara were two of a kind, only to him she had the face and body of a fairy-tale princess and he was an adoring frog. He was of medium height — half an inch less than six feet — of medium build, 175 pounds, but with a somewhat round face, a chin partially hidden by a flaccid neck and the marks of several years of severe acne. He was nobody's matinée idol, but he was also nobody's fool. Though not a quick wit, he was thoughtful and studious and held his own in late-night college bull sessions. He even rose to some distinction on occasion, once pushing through a handsome but somewhat less than popular fraternity pledge's acceptance by describing him as a "Beau Brummel of the boudoir."

Ernie was not good at social chitchat, but he had been the county declamation champion in his junior year of high school and had his photograph taken with a large trophy and published in the Selwin Daily Mirror. The next year he was elected president of his high school student body by putting his somewhat stilted speaking ability to good use, but more so perhaps by believing deeply in what he was proposing to do—to create a school radio station, open up the student government to more student involvement, and invigorate school spirit with bigger and better pep rallies—all high school stuff but all fairly important stuff to high school students.

That summer, before his senior year at Conners Hill High School, Ernie fell in love for the first time since he'd reached puberty and had become aware of beauty as it related to sex and sensuality. The object of his raging hormonal infatuation—love to those who believe love has anything to do with sex—was a junior and a majorette at Selwin's largest and most prestigious high school. With strong cheek bones, a perfectly formed body and legs that seemed to reach from the ground to her waist, she could have led the black-and-gold-clad marching band to hell and back without missing a beat, especially if all the members had been male. When she swung her legs into a high-stepping gait, the rhythm of Ernie's heart stepped up several dozen beats a minute and his mind lost all sense of rationality. The fact that she not only smiled at him but pressed her long legs against him and opened her moist, warm mouth to his probing tongue in the back seat of his best friend's car changed forever his perception of himself and the women he would come to know in the future.

Their relationship would also reveal the dark and dangerous side of Ernie's fragile self-image. Ultimately, he would become insanely jealous at the idea of losing her or even of living a week without her. His jealousy would exact the toll he feared. Needing her desperately, he wanted to know where she was every minute of the day, whom she talked to, why she was not at home when he called, where she had been, whom she had been with, why she thought they were worth her time and effort. He wanted to possess and dominate her life, and he wanted her to have no respect for anyone else's opinion but his own.

In short, Ernie Blaine wanted to be a slave master, and he soon gave the object of his affection no choice to be in a relationship with him. From that point on his desire to possess her in any way was doomed. Eventually he would learn that in life, as in abstract physics, every action has its immediate and opposite reaction and that when one perceives that one is trapped in a relationship, the first reaction is to escape.

The name of this long-legged majorette was Janine Carswell, and as with so many other women Ernie came to know and love as he grew older and wiser, he would forget neither her beautiful legs nor her beautiful smile. Nor would he forget the yellow-brown, corn-silk tassels of her hair, nor the deeply recessed pools of her black olive eyes. But those long legs perhaps became the symbol of everything he looked for in a beautiful woman from that moment on. Fifteen years later, nothing pleased Blaine more than to look at Vivian, his wife of ten years, and at her long, smooth, perfectly shaped legs and to understand that he had no idea why they were so beautiful. Baccara, Janine and Vivian all had the look of thoroughbred women: tall, statuesque and worthy of marble pedestals from which to look down and be admired by lesser mortals.

Ernie was a naturally adoring suitor. He had great admiration for most of the women in his life, even though he was constantly at odds with them for one reason or another. With his father gone most of the time, he had a mother, a grandmother and two sisters to contend with at home. They ran his life from almost the moment he was born until he left home for college and military service. And they were never far away. They talked constantly while he mostly sat and listened. They set the routines of family life by dominating the kitchen, the bathroom, the living room and the den with their chatter and their liveliness. Compared to them, Ernie was merely another household object. He seldom got a word in, and when he did, he was outclassed. The women in his family were natural communicators; he was an almost silent human being, a Trappist monk living in a convent of nattering nuns. He took refuge in athletics and reading and learned to love quiet, unassuming, thoughtful women. He discovered that they were internally the most passionate and the least predictable of all. They would always be the loves of his life.

Chapter 9

After court ended on the morning of the day Jesse had seen Vivian Blaine stumble from the car in front of her house, Stallings returned to the news office to begin writing a report of the legal proceedings. He was going over his notes when the phone on his desk rang. He picked it up and answered as usual.

"Jesse Stallings here."

"Mr. Stallings, this is Dave Devlin. You don't know me, but I read your editorials every now and then and I like the way you think. I was wondering if you would have time to speak to me privately if I came by the news office. I have something that might interest you."

"Certainly, Mr. Devlin. Any time, though I prefer a non-deadline day, say a Tuesday or Thursday, or even Saturday. That way I can talk without having to look at my watch every minute or so. That be okay with you?"

"Of course. Would you want to make it as early as tomorrow. I could come to your office around 9:30. Would that suit you?"

"That's fine. I'll see you tomorrow morning. In the meantime, could you give me a hint as to what you want to talk to me about? I do like to know a little something about what I'm getting into."

"Let's suffice it to say that I'm a private investigator and I've run across something that intrigues me. I thought you might be able to shed some light on the matter for me. It involves some local lawyers, a judge and a few members of the local police department. From your editorials and columns, I know that you have some contact with a good many of the businessmen and women in town and that you might be able to put some perspective on my observations."

"Sounds intriguing. I'm always interested in a good story, even if it's one I can't print. Come on down tomorrow and I'll see if I can be of any help."

After Stallings put down the phone, he whistled softly and exclaimed somewhat sarcastically: "Gee whiz, cops, lawyers and business types. What could they possibly have to do with one another?"

Hearing Jesse's comment through the partition that separated their office cubicles, McIan Dunbar, the News' sports editor, poked his head around the edge of the partition. "Sounds like you might have a live one on your hands, chief. Any chance I could listen in on the conversation? I'm always in the mood for a good mystery."

"Not yet, Mac. You know I'll let you in on what I know if I should know something, but right now all I know is that some P.I. says he's working on a case and has stumbled across some interesting information. I'm gonna talk to him tomorrow morning. When I know something, I'll fill you in—if, in fact, you need to know what I know.

Dunbar was Stallings' right-hand man. Though ostensibly a died-in-the-wool sports reporter and editor, he was more than a little interested in the machinations of politics and power, especially when they were related to business and pleasure. So was Jesse. That's what had gotten him into the newspaper business in the first place. He wanted to know what made society tick and who were the people who greased the wheels that made it run. In recent years, he had become convinced that technology, more than religion or philosophy or moral ethics, was the driving force of cultural revolutions. For a while it had been the steam engine, electricity, the locomotive, the automobile, the telephone, radio, television, and, of late, the personal computer. Other technologies had had their influence, of course, but the standouts had been those that generated great leaps in transportation and communication. They were the fluids that had greased the cylinders of business and social intercourse, that generated the conversations that led to the quest for more of everything, and ultimately to the frictions caused by the rapid intermingling of commercial, social and political forces.

As Dunbar stood behind and looked over his shoulder, Jesse reached out and clicked the browser icon on the computer monitor screen that opened his favorite Internet search engine. Into the single blank, Google space he typed the name "Dave Devlin," plus the phrase "private investigator, Conners Hill, NC." The first reference that appeared on the screen listed the P.I. as a member of the North Carolina Association of Private Investigators. It gave his business as "Devlin Investigative Services," along with a post office box number and telephone and fax numbers. Another search revealed that Devlin had once lived in Miami, Florida and perhaps some time at Carolina Beach on the North Carolina coast. A third listed him as a Certified Race Officer in a yacht club in St. Petersburg, Florida.

Surprisingly, Devlin's name also popped up in a reference to Writer's Digest, one of the nation's largest publishers of references to writers and publishing houses. Devlin had won an honorable mention for a mystery novel featuring Harry Paine, a P.I. who lived on a boat in the Miami area.

"Well, Mac, it looks like Mr. Devlin is a legitimate P.I. with an interesting background. Perhaps our talk tomorrow will be worth the time it takes," Jesse said.

"I hope so, Jesse. We need a little excitement around here. Maybe your Mr. Devlin will have something substantial. If not, at least he'll have an interesting story or two about what it's like to be a private investigator."

Chapter 10

Vivian Blaine awoke the morning after her "night on the town" with a splitting headache and a sour stomach. Too much booze and too many cigarettes had dulled her taste buds. The fuzz on her tongue tasted of stale, uncooked mushrooms and God only knew what else. She winced as she recalled some of the more lurid details of her playful good time in the back seat of the Mercedes. She had enjoyed it at the time but the memory was damning. Was she merely another woman without morals or scruples, or was there actually some redeeming social value to what she considered her mission in life? Was she merely destroying her life and her marriage—and perhaps the lives of her husband and children—in order to gain revenge against what she believed was the hypocrisy of her father's infidelities and his betrayal of her mother.

She remembered it all too well: the late night meals around the breakfast nook table in her family's home in

Greenville, the incessant beer drinking, the constant bickering, the smoldering cigarettes that hung from her mother's fingers until they seared the flesh and fell to the floor, her mother's endless cajoling of her father for his past sins, and finally her father's retreat to the downstairs bathroom where he would lock the door and pretend to read until he fell asleep. Her father would sometimes awaken at three or four in the morning, still sitting on the loosely hinged seat of the broken commode, still clad in his faded blue bathrobe and tattered bedroom slippers—still reeking of the eight or ten beers he had consumed between ten o'clock and midnight.

She recalled all too vividly the night she had awakened from a troubled sleep to find her mother standing over her with an upraised butcher knife.. "You little bitch," her bleary-eyed mother mumbled . "I know what you and your father have been up to. You can't fool me. I can see the way he looks at that little ass, the way he coddles you when he doesn't think I'm looking. He's a son-of-a-bitch and you're his little whore. Do you think I'm blind? Hell, no, I'm not blind. I know what's going on behind my back. I'm going to put a stop to it right now, while I still have my senses about me,"

Vivian had just celebrated her twelfth birthday the day before. Her father had invited half of the town's wealthiest families and their children to her party. He and several of his business associates had spent the previous night and most of the next day roasting a pig over a hickory-wood fire in a four-foot pit they had dug not twenty feet from the back door of the Beeler's two-story brick home. The men occupied themselves mostly by turning the pig, commenting on the progress of their work, drinking beer and telling jokes. Every now and then she went outside to watch the proceedings and listen to the stories. The men always told her how pretty she was and how fortunate she was to be her father's daughter. They said she was just as pretty as her mother and that she was getting to be a grown-up young woman. Vivian knew she was pretty and took their comments in stride, but she knew also that men often hid their true feelings.

"Your mom was a knockout back when she was in college," said Joe Smitherman to Vivian during one of her visits to the roasting pit. "Your dad was a lucky man to get his hands on such a prize. Why, if I'd been him, I wouldn't have let her out of my sight. I'd have locked her up and brought her out only for occasions like this. She's still a pretty woman though. Got a sharp tongue, but still a pretty woman. I bet half the men in this town would take her away in an instant if they thought they could get away with it."

Vivian looked at Smitherman and smiled sweetly Behind the smile was the thought that her father's friend was a fool. What kind of woman wants to be a prize possession? she thought. What kind of woman wants to be any kind of a possession? What good was being a knockout if it meant being treated like a piece of human furniture, like something to be admired not for its basic human value but as an object to be put on display? From that moment on, Vivian Beeler Blaine began to believe that while many men might be looked up to and admired, they could not be trusted to understand the meaning of true love and admiration.

By the time she was seventeen, Vivian had become what she thought she never wanted to be—a beautiful, coquettish young woman who loved being admired and sought after by the boys in her school. Much to her dismay, she had also become a woman in whose body the natural awakening of sexual appetite was reaching a perilous state. She felt herself more and more attracted to the young men who found her attractive not for her intellectual abilities but for the simple reason that she was beautiful and sexually desirable. She struggled constantly with the urges she felt to submit to their awkward advances and to let herself be overcome by the hormonal forces of her feminine nature, but she recognized that in the long run it would be a losing battle. Despite her precocious mind and her longing for spiritual solace, she knew that she was fighting a losing battle with her body. The intensity of her pounding heart and the heat of the flowing blood that sent torrents of tingling desire to every pour of her skin could not be denied. She attempted to slow the biological rush by engaging in every possible avenue of distraction. She joined the school band, the debate team, the Science Club and even the Future Farmers of America (after all, her father made his living selling farm equipment).

In the end, her last avenue of hope came from an unexpected source—a young man with above average intelligence and an ardent desire to become what he was not, a person of wealth and social status, one for whom no task would be too great to accomplish, no mountain too high to climb. Fortunately, he was good-looking and popular, with a muscled physique that came from long hours of work on the farm his father tended for a wealthy plantation owner. His high cheek bones, strong angular jaw and confident voice betrayed the quiet, well mannered introvert that Vivian found in him. Underneath, he was a boiling cauldron of ambition and desire, the greatest of which at the time was the longing to take Vivian into his arms and devour her with the ravenous force of a starving animal. It was only six months after they first began seeing each other that Vivian succumbed to the advances of her young Adonis in the back seat of her father's car. It was parked not twenty feet from the back door of her house, just above the spot where the pig-roasting had occurred on her twelfth birthday.

Chapter 11

Dave Devlin showed up at the Conners Hill News office on Thursday morning promptly at 9:30. As soon as he arrived and the receptionist had paged Jesse, the News' editor dropped what he was doing and headed for the front of the building. He walked down the L-shaped flight of stairs and over to the receptionist's desk to greet the P.I.

"Mr. Devlin?"

"Aye," said the affable investigator. He was wearing a light tan raincoat and a short-brimmed hat. The weather outside was clear but crisp. "I appreciate your taking the time to see me. I hope it won't be a waste of your time."

"No time is wasted if it leads to a good story, or even to a good lead," Jesse responded. "I'm glad you thought we might be able to be of some help, Mr. Devlin."

"Just call me Dave," said the P.I. "That's what my friends call me. I hope we might be friends."

Perfect Imperfection

"That's fine with me, and you can just call me Jesse. That's what most of my friends call me to my face. I'm sure they call me some other things at times, but that's the nature of this business. Would you like a cup of coffee before we go upstairs and get down to business?"

"Don't mind if I do," said Devlin. "It'll be my third one this morning, but a little caffeine helps keep the old ticker ticking."

"My sentiments exactly," said Jesse, knowing that his own six to eight cups of coffee a day did more than keep his heart beating. It kept him awake and occasionally on edge. His doctor had told him to lay off the caffeine, but it was a habit that was hard to break.

Jesse poured the hot black liquid into a Styrofoam cup. "Do you take sugar or cream?" he asked.

"No, I like it black. Keeps me from having to count too many carbohydrates."

"I'm afraid I stopped counting a long time ago," said Jesse. "In fact, I don't think I like coffee at all, but I like all the fattening stuff that goes in it. Dave, follow me to the conference room and we'll sit down where we can have a little privacy."

The two men walked the sixteen steps to the second floor and then down the right side of the building through the large editorial area to the conference room. They passed a couple of young advertising saleswomen on their way. The heavy wooden double doors into the meeting room were shut, but Jesse had made sure no one was planning to use it before going down to meet Devlin. Once inside, he closed the doors and asked Devlin to take a seat in one of six maroon, leather-bound chairs.

"This is a nice space for a paper this size," said Devlin. "You guys must do all right."

"Our publisher likes to give it some class," said Jesse. "It makes a good impression when we have to talk to politicians and professional people. Besides, the chairs are comfortable when staff meetings run long."

Jesse took a seat on the side of the large mahogany table opposite Devlin. "Now, Dave, why don't we get down to business? I believe you said you saw some things last night that intrigued you."

"Yeah. I get nervous when I see people in high places having late-night get-togethers. Makes me wonder what they're up to and whether it's all on the up and up. You know what I mean?"

"Certainly," said Jesse. "It's the same instinct reporters need if they're going to do their jobs well."

"I don't want to waste too much of your time, Jesse, so I'll get on with it. Here's what I was doing and what I saw that made me wonder what was going on last night!"

Devlin proceeded to lay out the reason for his following the plain-clothed Conners Hill policemen to the house on Willowgate Lane. He noted how he had recognized Chief Judge Feldman and a couple of attorneys but not the entourage of young women who arrived in the black limo. He explained how Feldman and the others stayed only a short time and left and then how two more men came out and got in the limousine with the very attractive blonde.

"Do you know whose house you were watching?" asked Stallings.

"No, but I'm sure it was somebody of importance. It was the only house in the cul-de-sac at the end of Willowgate Lane."

"Did anybody see you while you were there?"

"I don't think so; otherwise they might have confronted me about it."

"No doubt you're right," said Stallings. "In fact, a good way to put yourself under the scrutiny of the local police is to let them know you're putting them under some scrutiny. That isn't to say they are doing anything wrong, merely that they react the same way most of us react when we think someone is watching too closely. By the way, are you sure it was Judge Feldman you saw with the other lawyers?"

"I'm pretty certain," said Devlin. "I've been in district court a number of times when he was presiding. Although it was dark, I recognized him from his size and his walk—you know, the way he limps a little."

"Do you know how he got that limp?" Jesse asked.

"I think someone in court once told me he'd been wounded during the Vietnam War. That was about all I heard."

"Feldman got the limp during an attack on a Viet Cong machine-gun position. He was a second lieutenant leading his platoon up a hill when he stepped on a land mine. It blew off one of his legs and left the other one badly damaged. His determination to live was probably the thing that saved him. It's the same determination he exhibits as a judge, that and the fact that he has a passion for making fair and honest decisions."

"Are you saying you don't think there was anything underhanded going on while I was watching the house on Willowgate?"

"No, I'm not saying that. I'm merely saying that if there was anything out of line, I don't think Feldman was a part of it. I believe he's a reputable judge and that his reputation is well-earned. On the other hand, the house you were watching belongs to Sam Slocum, a real estate investor and big-time gambler. It's fairly well known that Slocum has political ambitions and that he's been thinking of running for a seat in the state legislature."

"What's his interest in politics? Wouldn't he be able to profit more as a local wheeler-dealer? Politics can put a spotlight on a businessman, especially if he's suspected of any questionable activity."

Jesse rubbed his balding head. "If it was just land development Slocum was interested in that might be the case, but what he's really passionate about, according to my sources, is legalized gambling. He wants to make gambling a state-condoned business operation. He wants to see the development of legal casinos across North Carolina."

"For what reason?"

"For public and private purposes. From what I hear, it's as much a personal psychological thing as a business interest. His father was a businessman who lost a fortune in the stock market crash of '29. He spent the rest of his life trying to earn back what he lost, but he never succeeded. He indoctrinated Sam with the idea that if one is going to gamble, it should be as the owner of the game, not as a mere player. Players win and lose but those who run the game always win. Besides that, he believes that to make winning a sure thing, the game must be a legal one."

Devlin smiled. "I see. That's where the lawyers and judges come in."

"You got it," said Jesse. "The legal system in this state is pretty much a good ol' boy association. Although most of the judges are elected by the people, the people usually go to the polls not knowing who the judicial candidates really are."

"Come to think of it, the last time I voted, I didn't see a single name on the ballot I recognized," Devlin admitted.

"There you go. The average voter doesn't know who the judicial bigwigs are because the lawyers and judges hand pick the people they want to run. They work from within the major political parties and the party faithful don't protest because the system has run fairly well for nearly two hundred years. They don't want to destroy the system; it has been too good to them. They're more or less like the rudder of a big ship. They're a seemingly small part of it, but they determine its ultimate direction. As for the system itself, the basic rule is the one every auto mechanic knows by heart: If it ain't broke, don't fix it."

"So the main goal of Slocum and his friends among the lawyers and judges is an attempt to tamper with the legal system?"

"Not just tamper with it but control it to some degree, to steer it in the direction they want it to go, at least on the issue of legal gambling. Although with Slocum, I suspect it's more than that. Some people would call it nothing more than a lust for power. It's mostly about the power of persuasion and that isn't illegal. Most of us just call it politics."

Devlin took note as Jesse reviewed the workings of the state's judicial-political setup. He realized that state judicial systems work as components of state government and that state governments rely heavily on the judicial systems to put their stamp of approval on the laws created by the politicians. It wasn't hard to see why lawyers and politics went hand in hand.

"One more question," said Devlin. "How do elections fit in all this? For instance, how does the governor fit into the equation?"

"The answer is simple," said Jesse. "He's a lawyer. So are most of the people who get elected to the states' highest political offices. An occasional outsider can make some waves and sometimes produce some real changes, but in a few short years, he's out on his ear and the system closes ranks again."

Devlin could not resist one more question. "You said 'he,' why not 'she'?"

"Oh, come on, Dave. When was the last time you heard of a woman being the governor of North Carolina? Never, that's when! Of course, in the last few years there has been a woman elected as lieutenant governor and one appointed as chief justice of the state's Supreme Court. The chief justice's appointment was no doubt one of political expediency, probably to keep the National Organization of Women from making a fuss in the state. But it did have an effect on the good ol' boy judicial system. And now we have a woman in the lieutenant governor's office, and she just might make it into the governor's office one day."

Devlin and Stallings ended their discussion with a plan to inform each other of any new developments concerning the party at Sam Slocum's house. Jesse wondered why Judge Phillip Feldman would consider meeting with Slocum at all, unless it was an attempt to find out just what Slocum was planning, or perhaps to lay the groundwork for his next campaign fund-raiser. For his part, Devlin was interested in the after-hours activities of Sgt. Alan Malloy, mostly because he had taken Anne Malloy's money to delve into the police officer's possible extra-marital relationship. Stallings and Devlin parted company on a high note, agreeing that a future meeting might be mutually advantageous.

Chapter 12

Devlin was right about several things. For one, Stallings' work as a reporter and editor had given the Conners Hill native an entry into the various levels of the social and cultural structure of the town. Over the years, the News' editor had sat in on numerous meetings of the local Chamber of Commerce, the Conners Hill Town Council, the community's five or six civic clubs, the board of directors of the Little Theatre, and, even the administrative meetings at a number of local churches.

He had written hundreds of stories about businesses and their owners, about startup business plans, employee retirement plans, health benefits, profit-sharing and profit-taking. He had watched as aspiring young politicians entered the race for seats on the town council, the planning board, the zoning board of adjustment, the library board and the public safety oversight board. Invariably, he found most of them to be well-meaning and idealistic. Occasionally, he found one to be more interested in personal advancement than in the overall public good. Inevitably, such ambition was as obvious as it was awkward. Such candidates always seemed to be running for the next position beyond the one he or she claimed to be seeking. Jesse could see it in their eyes and hear it in their voices. It would come from an assistant district attorney ostensibly running for the D.A.'s office but looking ahead to become a Superior Court judge, or a town council candidate with his eye on the mayor's office or that of a state representative.

Jesse didn't fault ambitious young men and women for looking and planning ahead, unless their ambition got in the way of the performance of the duties of the office they had won. In fact, one of his favorite politicians always seemed to be running for the next rung on the political ladder. Stallings had met him when he was a young elementary school teacher working toward becoming a member of the local school board. When he was elected to the board, he began running for a position as a county commissioner. Later, he sought the job of a representative in the state legislature. Most astute political observers believed his ultimate goal was to become the governor and perhaps a U.S. senator. Somewhere along the way, his plans went awry and he found himself licking his political wounds. A few men and women had achieved their long-range goals not by ambition alone but by doing their jobs to the best of their abilities. It was always a relief when candidates with more ambition than ability reached their level of incompetence and wound up as an illustration of

The Peter Principle. Oftentimes after that, their careers stalled or took a downhill slide into political oblivion.

Jesse's favorite politicians were the ones who seemed to be running only for the right to serve the public, who wanted to be true public servants. They were not the "do-gooders" so much as the "good-doers," those who felt they could make a real difference in the lives of the average citizens of the community. Fortunately, there were perhaps more of them than the public deserved. They operated mostly in the political background, frequently took low-profile jobs and did what needed to be done. More often than not they eschewed the fact that they had been instrumental in helping make local government work.

Jesse believed he understood the pretenders well because he had once been one of them. As a reporter, he had wanted to be an editor; as an editor, he wanted to be a managing editor; as a managing editor he wanted to be a part of the newspaper ownership. Only after it became apparent that the latter was not in the realm of possibility at the Conners Hill News did he come to understand that he wanted the position of a reporter with the status of an owner.

Then one day it came to him. A voice in his head chimed in loud and clear: "You are somebody," it said. "Be who you are."

After that, Jesse's place in the scheme of things became remarkably clear. He was a reporter, photographer and editor. His only role was to do his job as best he could—to do what needed to be done and forget the rest. In the end, it had been a formula for success and happiness. At age 55, he found himself both successful and happy. He had a house that was paid for, enough money in stocks and bonds to allow him to retire with a reasonable degree of comfort, a wife and two children who were relatively prosperous and content, and a feeling that he had achieved a fair amount of respect in the community.

Nonetheless, Stallings also felt himself to be an outsider in the town he had grown up in, moved away from and then moved back to as an aspiring young journalist. His job as a reporter and editor put him in the middle of much of what was going on in the town, but his meager salary kept him out of some of the financial planning and governance that are essential elements of high level municipal development. He knew most of what went on in the public meetings and sometimes in private business conclaves, but the wheeling and dealing that were often essential parts of large economic projects showed up for him only as shadowy hints of what lay behind such projects.

For instance, he knew how Sam Slocum had made his money in the real estate business, but he did not know well the friends and associates who were Slocums' investors and financial partners. He associated with them in public but not in private. They were essential elements of Slocum's success; however, to Stallings as well as the general public, they remained mostly anonymous and sometimes frighteningly ominous despite their small-town, good ol' boy appearances.

Jesse also knew that the banking community was a major element of any successful real estate venture. Banks and bankers had access to untold millions of dollars stored away in their vaults for safekeeping and investment opportunities of their customers. Technically, the banks operated under strict state and federal regulations. Nonetheless, practically speaking they were able to dole out funds for nearly any purpose they deemed appropriate—provided they could protect the loans with rigorous collections and secure collateral based on real property or other valuable assets, like stocks or bonds.

At least one close friend of Slocum's was a bank president who was known for making shrewd deals with start-up companies that appeared to have both good management and good growth potential. It was rumored that the banker was a liberal lender but one whose lending policies came with an unwritten, seemingly-unorthodox and possibly illegal condition: that in addition to the normal fees and interest on the bank's loans, the bank's president was to receive a percentage of the profits of the company over the life of the loan. In other words, the lender was to become a kind of silent partner in the business. It was a stipulation many potential borrowers found repugnant and unethical, although from everything Stallings could learn, it was standard operating procedure for so-called venture capitalists. The problem in Jesse's mind was that when a bank president became a venture capitalist he was using his customers' money, not his own, as the venture capital. Nonetheless, according to Jesse's sources, some of whom were recipients of the local bank's "generosity," the practice went on for years until it got the attention of state bank auditors and suddenly came to an end.

CHAPTER 13

Even in the worst of times, Vivian Blaine believed she was control of her life. She had graduated from Grandboro College with honors, had been a member of the student judicial board and a popular actress with the GC theater troupe. She was looked up to and often emulated by her female classmates, who found her outgoing and unpretentious though occasionally a little withdrawn. Despite her popularity and her ability to put on a good face in almost any situation, she sometimes suffered from mood swings that approached the edge of depression. When that happened, she immersed herself in her books and studied them with the intensity of a scientist on the scent of a new discovery. Or she pretended to be even more the extrovert than most of her classmates believed she was in fact. She would become the life of a party, the girl for whom life itself was a seemingly never-ending merry-go-round of shallow ups and downs in which the ups always canceled out the downs.

Often at least one of her tactics provided the desired result. During her withdrawal stages she frequently came away with some new insight into her tortured past, some rationale as to why she suffered the slings and arrows of a painful childhood or perhaps with a new resolve gleaned from the words of some poet whose life she believed to be similar to her own. It was from her reading that she came away not only with hope but with the conviction that "life is fatal but not serious"—that life is, after all, merely "a sexually transmitted dis-ease." During one of her periods of contrasting hope and despair, she stumbled upon a book of Epicurean philosophy entitled Life Is Uncertain: Eat Dessert First!

The title itself fit neatly into her growing belief that a healthy appetite not only for food but for all things sensual was not only a means to an end but an end in itself. One might die of obesity, alcoholism or even of an infectious disease, but the time would not be wasted in the belief that the well-lived life is one of rigid austerity and discipline. Like a big-bellied, laughing Buddha, she believed a full life was one in which the opposites of good and evil were not opposites at all, but merely opposite ends of a stick used to stir the soup of physical and psychological existence. Emily Dickinson was one of her favorite poets, and Dickinson had expressed the thought succinctly when she wrote: "I burn my candle at both ends; it cannot last the night. But oh, my foes, and ah, my friends, it gives a lovely light!" By the end of her junior year in college, Vivian had decided she would burn her candle at both ends.

Perfect Imperfection

With full lips, high cheekbones, a cleft chin and curvaceous figure, she was the envy of many young women who were less well-endowed both mentally and physically. Unlike most of them, she believed God had a purpose for her life that exceeded her single, solitary existence in the stream of time. Unfortunately she believed God's purpose for her was both a blessing and a curse—a blessing that her ultimate destiny was timeless, a curse that there was only so much earthly time to discover it.

In a constant state of flux between two extremes, Vivian's personality wavered from one side of an ideal emotional equilibrium to the other. One minute she was calm, relaxed and self-controlled. The next minute she was excited, anxious and self-deprecating. The periods of flux varied from as little as a hour to a month, perhaps even six months. But no matter what their length or what their direction, at some point they came to an end, reversing their direction and their strength. Even in her happiest moments, when her gleaming teeth showed through smiling lips, one could see a sadness behind the smile. It was as if the smile masked a vague memory of some inexpressible pain.

When Ernie first met Vivian he was suffering from the gnawing pain of his on-again, off-again relationship with Baccara Thomason. He had met Baccara when she was a senior in college and he had fallen hopelessly in love with her on their first date. But over a period of nearly six years, she had driven him to despair by going out with what seemed to him a parade of young professional men, mostly doctors and lawyers. He had proposed marriage to her at least twice, but with her mind set on an idyllic life with a man of means, she had turned him down each time. Only after he had announced to her that he had been accepted at the University of North Carolina's School of Law did she consent to his third proposal. By then, however, it was too late. During one of his fits of despair and before he had made up his mind to attend the law school, he had consented to meet and go out with Vivian.

"What would you like to do?" Ernie had asked when he called her for a date.

"The county fair is in town," she responded immediately. "Let's go to the fair. We can wear jeans and be comfortable."

Her lack of hesitation was both refreshing and startling, far different from any response he would have gotten from Baccara.

"Would you like to go out and get something to eat first?" Ernie had asked.

"No. We can get a hot dog or some Polish sausage at the fair. It'll be fun."

Ernie was elated. At last he had met a girl who did not have to be impressed on the first date. It would be only one of many welcome surprises that would come from the seemingly casual but elegant blond-haired beauty.

He picked her up at Grandboro College around 6:30 p.m. on a Saturday evening. She was wearing denim jeans, a dark red sweatshirt and scuffed white running shoes. She had made a ponytail of her flowing blond hair by tying it up with a dark red bow. Ernie's aunt had told him Vivian was attractive, but she had given no indication of just how attractive. When she came downstairs to meet him in the parlor of the college dorm, he was astounded. He had described himself to her when he called and when she saw him, she bounded up to him and gave him a hug as if he were a long-lost love.

"Hi, Ernie. I'm Vivian," she said with a broad grin. "You ready to go?"

Ernie decided at that moment that he would be ready to go almost anywhere with her. Little did he know where anywhere might be.

He walked her to his car, which was parked near the GC dorm. Before he could open the passenger-side door for her, she had already climbed in. He went to the driver's side, opened his door and got into the driver's seat. On the way to the fair, she asked him how his aunt was, how she had come to suggest that he call her, and whether he really liked going to the fair or was just trying to please her.

"I love fairs," said Ernie. "Not so much for the rides or the sideshows but for the crowds. I love watching the people. I guess I'm a voyeur at heart."

"We have something in common then," said Vivian. "I'm a people person, too. I'm always trying to figure out what makes them tick. I guess I think if I find out, I'll find out what makes me tick as well."

Ernie believed he had found a soul-mate. He didn't know much about what made people tick, but he knew that already Vivian had caused his heart to skip a beat or two.

At the end of their two-hour visit to the fair, Blaine believed he had learned more about Vivian Beeler than he had learned about Baccara Thomason in three years of on-and-off dating. He knew Vivian liked hot dogs with mustard and chili, that the deep-fat-fried, sugar-sprinkled dough called funnel cake was one of her weaknesses, and that she could eat, walk and talk as comfortably as she dressed. On the way back to the dorm, she suggested they stop at a popular drive-in restaurant called Ham's.

"Do you drink beer?" asked Ernie.

"Not really," Vivian replied. "I inhale it."

She told the truth in an odd sort of way. She didn't really like the taste of beer, but she loved the way she felt after downing two or three in succession. She said it loosened her inhibitions and made her breathe more freely. "It's the same as loosening your bra when you've dressed to impress someone you really don't want to impress," she explained.

"Did you do that tonight?" asked Ernie.

"I'm not wearing a bra," said Vivian. "See," she said as she reached out, took his hand and slipped it under her sweatshirt. Her breasts were firm and taut and perfectly formed. "From what you said to me on the phone, I knew I didn't have to impress you."

"What did I say on the phone?"

"You said your aunt said I was a nice girl and you wanted to find out for yourself."

"And that meant you didn't have to impress me?"

"No, it meant that you hadn't formed any preconceived notions of me and that you were willing to let me be me."

"And are you you?"

She pressed his hand to her chest again. "What do you think?" she asked.

Chapter 14

Jesse Stallings did not mention it to Dave Devlin, but the day before Devlin had followed Alan Malloy to the gathering at Sam Slocum's house, Jesse had received an invitation to a dinner meeting at the Slocums. It took him by surprise, as he and Slocum, though casual acquaintances, were not close friends. Jesse ran into Slocum at various business and social functions, including the annual Conners Hill Chamber of Commerce banquet, the Rotary Club pancake suppers, and occasionally during a downtown street festival. Slocum was always friendly and cordial. Occasionally they exchanged a colorful joke or two, but their conversation rarely went beyond mere social protocol. Even so, Jesse knew from his conversations with other local businessmen that Slocum had a flair for making money and a love of doing so by taking calculated risks. One of his real estate deals had gone awry and had landed him in hot water both with the county's tax office and the local Realtor's Association. He had managed to slip out of the quandary and keep his head above water. Had he not been able to back up his claim that he was involved in the deal merely as a broker rather than a buyer, he might have ended up with a revoked real estate license and a six-month jail term.

Once Jesse learned who were the other guests invited to the Slocums' dinner, he knew why he and Janice were also invited. The guest list included Robert Ziglar, mayor of Conners Hill; Lawrence Cameron, head of a local trucking company; Cletus Lampley, president of the Northern Fidelity Bank; and Kingston Armor, another real estate investor. Also invited was Pat Tomlinson, a lawyer and former mayor. All were active in the community through the Chamber and through various churches and civic clubs. Lawrence Cameron had once been a Realtor but had left the business after making several deals that the Realtor's Association had found "questionable." Not long afterward, he and his wife split up and he took over a national trucking company franchise.

Dinner was to be held at eight that evening. Stallings' wife Janice was feeling somewhat fidgety before the two of them left for the party. She asked Jesse to zip up the back of her long black dress before she put on the matching sequined jacket

"Why did you say Sam Slocum's wife wanted us to come to this affair?" she asked demurely. "I don't really know her very well, and I didn't think you and Sam were all that close either"

Perfect Imperfection

"To tell you the truth, Jan, I really don't know why we are invited, except for what the invitation said, but I can imagine several scenarios. Of course, you know Judith Slocum wants the wives there to discuss a project to acknowledge some of the older women of the community."

"Oh, yes, I read the invitation. Judith said she wants to talk about planning and preparing a Christmas party for the widows of several deceased businessmen. It sounds like a very good idea. A lot of those women were as much a part of their husbands' successes as their husbands. As I understand it, some of them had more to do with their husbands' success than their husbands."

"Now, Janice. Don't be coy. You may know that to be the case, but I wouldn't push it too far."

"Jesse, you know me better than that. I never push anyone too far. In fact, I never push at all. I believe in standing by my husband, not behind him."

It was something Stallings appreciated more than his wife knew. In fact, the only time she ever pushed him was if she wanted him to take a firmer hand with their two children. She was often frustrated with the fact that because he was so often at work, both day and night, she ended up being the voice of authority when it came to the kids. Jesse never felt that his not being there was a fatal flaw in their upbringing. After all, his own father had been gone most of the time and Jesse had turned out all right. Of course, his grandmother had been the authority figure in their household. She was a lady who thought of herself as a "grand dame" of the community and often said so.

Jesse finished zipping up his wife's dress and continued speculating as to why he was invited to the party. Janice appeared not be listening, but as always she heard every word and stored it in her subconscious along with all the other things that she would one day drag out and used both to his and her benefit.

Jesse continued his rambling. "My guess is that Slocum wants to talk about the future of development in the town and perhaps to sound out the Mayor and others on his notion to bring casino gambling to the state. He knows that if he's going to get anywhere at all with the idea, he'll need the approval, or at least the acceptance, by the major players in his own community. Sam may be a lot of things, but he's no fool. He knows one of the major ways of affecting a community's thinking is to get the local press on his side. I guess the best way to start currying the favor of the press is to invite the local newspaper editors to dinner."

"Sounds like a good idea to me," said Janice. "Of course, you would never do anything that would cast doubt on your integrity. Right, Jesse?"

"Oh, Jan, you know me better than I know myself."

"And just what does that mean?

"It means you know when I'm lying and when I'm telling the truth."

"I know you don't lie, Jesse. But I know you might be susceptible to a little shading of the truth."

"You think so?"

"I know so!"

Chapter 15

The Stallings arrived at the Slocum residence a little later than the other guests. Sam and Judith Slocum met them at the front door and greeted them graciously. To Jesse, the home seemed larger than he had remembered. The large colonial-style brick house was more impressive the closer he got to it. Once inside, it seemed he had entered a modern-day castle. The vaulted story-and-a-half foyer ceiling seemed twice as high as it was, and the light from the crystal chandelier hanging nearly fifteen feet above his head produced a speckled dance on the black and gray slate floor.

"Welcome to our modest abode," said Sam Slocum as he stuck out his hand to Jesse. "We are delighted to have the two of you join us tonight. It's unfortunate that we don't get to see more of you than we do."

Judith Slocum, a tall, willowy blonde dressed in fashionable black slacks and a deep purple silk blouse, was even more effusive. "How good to see you, Janice," she said as she wrapped her arms around Jesse's wife and gave her a warm embrace. "It's been ages since we've had the chance to get together."

Janice Stallings couldn't recall when she'd ever been together with Judith, who at thirty-seven looked almost ten years younger than she was. But Janice was taken with the younger woman's lithe figure and seemingly flawless complexion. She took special note of the long blond hair that was pulled back into a ponytail and held in place by an ornate silver ring encrusted with diamonds.

"Most of the others are already in the den having a drink and an appetizer," Sam announced. "Follow me and we'll go back and join them. Dinner won't be ready for another thirty minutes or so. I know the two of you know most everybody here, so you'll feel right at home, I'm sure."

In the den Jesse felt more at home than Janice, although she was the one from the family whose fortunes came closer to the Slocums' than the Stallings'. Through his work at the newspaper Jesse had come to know most of the town's wealthier citizens and to appreciate both their fortunes and their foibles. And though he admired both their style and their substance, he had no desire to live as they undoubtedly did, surrounded by beautiful architecture, beautiful furnishings and better than average-looking people. He was usually comfortable with the knowledge that he lived more in his head and heart than in his surroundings. Nonetheless he was occasionally a little envious of the elegant lifestyle of the town's well-to-do.

"Ladies and gentlemen, thank you for being here tonight," Sam Slocum said after announcing the Stallings arrival. "I know you all are wondering what is on the agenda, but I can assure you that there is nothing sinister. Judith and I mostly wanted to get to know all of you better and to express our appreciation for the influence and effect you have had on the town of Conners Hill. Without your devotion and dedication, as well as your expertise…and no doubt a lot of your money…this town would not be in the ideal position it is today.

"Now those of you who know me well also know that I seldom do anything without a purpose that involves both your expertise and your money. You know I would be lying if I said otherwise, but I can assure you that what I am up to is something that will benefit all of us, not just Judith and I, but all of you here tonight as well as the general population of the town. As much as I believe Conners Hill is the geographical center of the region and that we have a destiny to become its financial and social heart as well, I believe we can advance our cause rather dramatically in the near future. I know you want to do everything you can to make our vision of the future as bright as it can possibly be.

"And now, before I bore you to death, let's proceed to the dining room and enjoy our meal. Judith, if you will show the ladies the way, I'll tag along with the gentlemen." Sam turned to the five or six men. "I don't know about you, boys, but I'm starved. Let's see what the little woman has prepared."

Chapter 16

The dining room and the table were large enough to seat the Slocums and all their guests comfortably. The meal, served by waiters in white, cut-off jackets, was exquisite. Aperitifs of dry French vermouth and hors d'oeuvres of scallops wrapped in peppered bacon had been served in the den and had accomplished their purpose of whetting the guests' appetites. Once seated, the group was served a Mediterranean bisque consisting of a blend of rich, creamy tomatoes topped with mozzarella cheese and garnished with fresh mint and lemon. Next came a choice of almond crusted chicken breasts with peaches, blueberries, and a grand marinade, or oven-roasted halibut drizzling with champagne cream and garnished with spiced pecans.

"How do you do it?" the wife of one of the guests asked Judith Slocum when the first course had been served.

"How do I do what?" Judith replied.

Perfect Imperfection

"How do you manage to put together such a lovely meal and remain so calm and relaxed? I would have been a nervous wreck if I had had to prepare this and entertain all of us?"

"Oh, it's quite simple," said Judith. "It's just a matter of knowing what you want and how to get it. The truth is I was born on a farm and I'm still a simple country girl. But I know what makes the men folk happy. I just decide what they like and then I order out."

A small rivulet of tomato bisque trickled down the chin of Kingston Armor as he grinned at Judith's remark. It was obvious from most of the males around the table that Judith knew what men liked and how to procure it.

Not all the businessmen's wives were amused, though few, if any, showed the tension they felt. One felt obliged to change the subject to something a little less threatening.

"Judith, tell us a little bit about the project you have planned for the widows of some of our former businessmen," she said.

"Oh, that will come after dessert," said Judith. "It's something I've been planning for a long time, something I think all of you will appreciate."

The dessert was as mouth-watering as the main course. Consisting of white chocolate amaretto cheesecake with strawberries and whipped cream and followed with cups of steaming black coffee, it filled most of the guests with warm, pleasant sensations.

Chapter 17

After the meal, Sam Slocum invited the men to join him in his study, while the women followed Judith back to the den to begin their discussion of their get-togethers for some of the town's older women. Judith laid out her plans with the same directness she used in her entertaining. She came right to the point and then asked for recommendations or suggestions from the other wives. She never questioned whether the project should be done, only how and when it should be done. In her mind, it was already an accomplished fact. It needed only the assent and enrollment of the women who would assist her.

"I've been thinking that perhaps it would be good to begin with two of these a year," said Judith as she outlined the purpose and planning for the event. "Perhaps once at Christmas and once sometime in the spring, maybe as a patio picnic or garden party. What do you think?"

"How many people are you considering having at the event?" asked Marjorie Cameron. "I'm not sure all of us have the space or the culinary skills required to put it together as well as you do."

"Well, since I am trying to initiate the project, I propose to make it a luncheon party and have it here for at least a year or two. After that, we can decide if we want to hold it somewhere else. I thought maybe we would start with ten to twenty guests. Sam and I both enjoy having people over, and we are especially happy if we can do something for our business widows."

Emma Jean Lampley, wife of Cletus Lampley, was enthusiastic. "I'm all for it," she said. "I would be happy to help out in getting the affair started. Who knows, maybe one day one of us will be attending the luncheon as guests. It would be awfully nice to know that someone remembered us and was thinking of us and what we and our husbands had meant to the town."

"I second that," chimed in Faith Ziglar. "Most people don't know what goes on in the background of business or politics. It ain't all that glamorous all the time. People don't understand the sacrifices that are made by the wives and children of businessmen and politicians. Of course, I know about politics more than business. In fact, I know more than I ever wanted to know. A politician's wife is about as low on the totem pole as a snake in the grass. We do half the work and our husbands get all the glory. You can sign me up right now."

Janice Stallings said she thought the project was worthwhile and that she could imagine numerous benefits to come from it. "I'm sure Jesse would be happy to give the event some publicity once it gets started," she said.

"We aren't doing this to get our names in the paper," said Judith, "but we all know that a little publicity doesn't hurt. In fact, just knowing that someone is doing something for someone else may give others in the community an idea or two for joining in. You never know what will become of a good thing once it's begun."

In the study, the conversation was taking a different tact. Sam Slocum was as direct in his dealings with others as his wife, though his motives were not always quite as pure. Once he had passed out the Cuban cigars and offered a brandy to each of the men, Sam came right to the point.

"Let me be clear about this, gentlemen. I asked you here tonight to bend your ear a little and to see what you think about my proposal to establish casino gambling in North Carolina. Before I begin, I know that all of you are well-established Christian businessmen who want no part of anything that would bring dishonor to yourselves or the town. I also know that as businessmen, you sometimes must make difficult decisions in order to keep your businesses afloat. But most important of all, we must all operate with one basic principle in mind: our revenues must be greater than our expenses. We have to earn more than we spend to make our businesses work. That's the bottom line. I assume that as successful managers you all agree with that."

Sam waited for each man to signal his approval, which most did with a mere nod of the head. Then he continued his pitch.

Perfect Imperfection

"My purpose in having you here tonight—besides wanting you to enjoy yourselves—is to ask you to listen to my ideas about the casino business and discuss the pros and cons of legalizing casino gambling in the state. All I ask is that you listen and consider the facts. I will not be offended if you disagree with what I have in mind. In fact, I hope some of you will disagree in order that I might see some of the negative rationale I have not seen before. I don't want to jump into some venture in which the disadvantages outweigh the advantages. I want to engage in a project that is good for all those who are involved in it. And, actually, not just for those involved in it, but for the general population as well. The question is: will you hear me out?"

Chapter 18

The men in the study of the Slocum house turned very quiet at Sam's request. The stillness was not engendered so much by the request as by the very mention of the word gambling. It was not something that most men of sound business sense considered practical, much less prudent. Gambling was just that, gambling—taking a chance with one's money that more often than not was extremely risky and unwise, and, in some cases, decidedly unhealthy. Gambling involved risking one's money on the chance that things might turn out well. Business, on the other hand, involved taking risks not dependent totally on chance. It involved taking calculated risks based on knowledge and wisdom and the willingness to work hard to bring about the desired results. Even if one's business sense was flawed, the willingness to work could often turn the risks into profit. Many men with little or no practical business experience had become successful through sheer effort, will power and hard work. Human character, not chance, was the main ingredient of a successful business venture. Such was the general attitude of the men Slocum had invited to share a meal and their thoughts on his pet project.

"Sam, I hate to say this, but I believe you may be asking us to consider something most of us here tonight have little affinity for," said Kingston Armor. "Sure, we all like to play poker occasionally, and no doubt some of us will wager a little money on an ACC basketball game or perhaps even place a bet on a horse or a dog when we're on vacation, but staking a lot of capital or our reputations on a gambling operation is not something most of us would consider reasonable. We're businessmen, not gamblers."

"I agree one hundred percent," said Robert Ziglar. "Conners Hill has built a fine reputation as a town that respects wealth and good fortune, but it respects health and hard work even more. A town's reputation as a place where people want to live and work and send their children to school is more important than the financial interests of its wealthiest residents. It's been my experience that people who've made the most money in the least amount of time often leave town to go and live in places with other wealthy people. They don't generally relish the character and flavor of small town people so much as the value of their own self-importance. In my mind, professional gambling attracts a bad lot, and gambling with professionals results in a few winners and a lot of losers."

"Here, here," chimed in Greg Irwin, owner of a recreational vehicle dealership and a dedicated church leader. "Turning a town into a haven for professional gambling is like turning a restaurant into a bar for alcoholics. You end up with a lot of poor players and pitiful drunks. I'm totally opposed to gambling on its face. It isn't something America can be proud of. Just look at the places that have fallen for it. There may be a lot of glitz on the so-called "strip," but there's a whole lot of pitiable people in the alleys and side streets begging for handouts. As far as I'm concerned, a casino is the devil's playground, bar none."

Chapter 19

Sam Slocum realized prior to inviting his guests for dinner that he would run into some strong opposition to his plan. However, he was not the kind of man to let small obstacles deter him. In fact, obstacles were often what kept him going. They were challenges to be met and overcome, temporary breakdowns that caused one's determination to grow stronger.

Slocum liked to say that breakdowns were an essential ingredient of breakthroughs. "One can't get through, over or around a wall until one gets to it," he had preached to several of his business associates. "The wall is merely a barrier that causes one to pause, ponder, reflect and reconsider the possibilities of creating breakthroughs."

The philosophy had always worked well for him. Even when he ran into real estate problems, he decided it was an opportunity rather than an obstacle. He merely changed course and pursued his ultimate goal as if it were a temporary setback, which, indeed, it was.

John Staples

Sam didn't care how much verbal opposition he faced as long as the majority of those from whom he sought money or advice gave it in the end. He was certain that most of the men who opposed gambling on moral grounds would not oppose it on economic grounds. He had done his homework and he was ready for whatever was thrown at him. He was anxious to begin his pitch.

"Let me ask you gentlemen one simple question," Sam said, waiting for either a yea or a nay. When no one spoke up, he continued.

"When do you think legal gambling began in this country? Would you say it was more than a hundred years ago, say in the late 1800s or so? Or was it before that?"

"What has this got to do with whether North Carolina should have casinos?" asked Irwin. "Gambling has been around for thousands of years. Roman soldiers gambled for Jesus' cloak at his crucifixion. Wherever there's people, there's gambling, but that doesn't make it right."

Nods came from all around the room.

"I agree, gentlemen," said Sam. "But the question is not a rhetorical one. Perhaps you're not aware of it, but there has been legalized gambling in America since early colonial days. Not everybody approved of it, of course, especially the Puritans. But many settlers who were not Puritans had no problems with it. In fact, among those settlers, gambling was considered a mostly harmless diversion.

"Believe it or not, every one of the original thirteen colonies had established lotteries to raise revenues for public works projects. Many of the earliest and most prestigious universities—Harvard, Yale, Princeton,

Dartmouth, William and Mary and others—garnered proceeds from government-run lotteries. Gambling funds were even used to build churches and libraries. Benjamin Franklin, John Hancock and George Washington were known to have sponsored some of the lotteries for public works programs.

"Of course, there were critics and skeptics back then. Some English financiers suspected that gambling was the principal cause of the colonies' inability to sustain themselves without British help. Once the fight for independence began, the Continental Congress enacted a provision for a $10 million lottery to finance the war. It was later abandoned as grandiose and ineffective."

"Looks like you've done your homework, Sam," said Kingston Armor, "but what's the point? No matter how prevalent or established gambling has been, in this day and time it still has the taint of the underworld, if not the devil himself. How're you gonna sell the public on the idea that casino gambling is a legitimate business enterprise—especially here in the South where our religious heritage is still the foundation of society?"

"I'm glad you asked that," Sam responded. "It's a good question and one that deserves some serious discussion. First of all, since you mentioned the South, let me remind you that although we have a deep-seated religious heritage, we also have a history of being open to all sorts of gaming operations. Our attitudes have pretty much reflected the traditions of the various Spanish, French and other national and ethnic traditions. We all know about Mississippi riverboat gamblers and poker games played in the back rooms of saloons and country clubs. And we know that

New Orleans was once the gambling capital of the nation. And then there's the universal hobby of betting on sports. Not only that, but many of you here tonight have bought tickets to everything from the Conners Hill Little Theatre drawing to the Lions Club automobile raffle."

"I'll admit that many of us have been involved in such fund-raisers," said Robert Ziglar. "Church bingo and civic club raffles are one thing, but they're a far cry from organized gambling. They're local and controllable, while casinos, no matter who runs them, are big-time operations and control is haphazard at best."

"Undoubtedly that was true in the beginning," said Sam. "It's no secret that organized crime syndicates were early supporters of gaming operations and were heavily invested in them. We all know that the Mafia was a major source of capital for the development of Las Vegas, and that many of the early casinos there were run by crime syndicates. We've all seen the movies and heard the horror stories about the Mafia, but what isn't generally known today is the degree to which casino gambling has become a well-controlled, legitimate business enterprise. That's because Congressional investigations during the nineteen fifties resulted in a crackdown and a cleansing of the casino industry. Eventually, the mob was forced out and ended up selling their casino interests to lawful businessmen and publicly-traded companies. If you want proof of that, take a look at all the stories in Forbes magazine that have been written within the last year. You'll find that casino gambling has become one of the most highly regulated industries in America."

"What's the basis of that opinion?" asked Greg Irwin.

Sam Slocum, as always, had a ready answer. "For one thing," said Slocum, "most all casino companies today are publicly-held corporations, with common names like Hilton, Sheraton and TW. They are answerable to their stockholders, the thousands of individual investors who own the stock. For another, they are answerable to the federal Securities and Exchange Commission, which regulates all major publicly held corporations. In addition, they are licensed and tightly regulated by state and local governments. Lastly but perhaps most importantly, they are run by legitimate businessmen using all the tools of the business world: accountants, attorneys, payroll specialists, auditors and market researchers. Their sole purpose is to make a decent profit, not to fleece the unsuspecting public."

"You make a good case," said Irwin, "but isn't it still a fact that wherever there is large-scale gambling, there are all kinds of openings for unscrupulous opportunists to make money through less than desirable means. For instance, isn't it true that when you have hundreds or perhaps thousands of gamblers in a town, many of them will become addicted to the habit and will end up poor, desperate and sometimes unstable? And don't they often become the victims of unscrupulous pawnbrokers and other kinds of moneylenders? I still believe anything that contributes to such circumstances is ultimately a bad deal."

Slocum felt the discussion was taking a negative turn and deftly ended his pitch to his guests. Jesse Stallings had not offered a word during the proceedings, but he was aware of Slocum's intent, which was merely to put his chips on the table and see who wanted a piece of the action. Slocum had opened a small crack in some very closed minds and he would in the days to come fill it with enticingly lucrative propositions. He had accomplished his mission of assessing the opinions of the town leaders and of determining who would be his helpers and who would oppose him.

Chapter 20

As they left the Slocum residence that night, Jesse Stallings and his wife followed a gaggle of husbands and wives along the long driveway to their automobiles. Stallings hardly followed the conversations of the group until he heard someone utter a familiar name.

"Did you hear about Vivian Blaine?" one woman said to another.

"No, what about her?" asked the other. "I don't know her really. She seldom comes to church with Ernie. He's a very nice fellow and a good husband from what I hear."

"Everyone seems to think so," said the first, but I've heard that Vivian treats him like dirt. She acts like he's not good enough to be her husband, much less the father of her children. You'd think a brazen woman like that would learn that all that glitters isn't gold. Ernie's a solid citizen, but from what I've heard, you'd think Vivian married him just to get three meals a day and a roof over her head. But that's not my concern anyway. I heard last night at the bridge club that she had disappeared."

The entire entourage of spouses abruptly halted. The men looked as puzzled as the women and perhaps a bit more concerned.

"What do you mean 'disappeared'?" asked Robert Ziglar's wife, Hope. "You mean she hasn't been seen in The Coffee Spoon in the past week, or what?"

"No, I mean 'disappeared' as in 'poof, gone, obliterated from the world.' I mean no one has seen or heard anything from her for a week. A neighbor of theirs told me Ernie is absolutely beside himself with grief. He's had to make arrangements for an aunt or someone to take care of the kids. There's been no word from anyone about where Vivian may be or who she may be with."

"What's that supposed to mean?" said Hope Ziglar. "Is there some reason she might have left town with someone, like on a vacation or something? She has a secretarial job at Wolf Johnson's office, doesn't she? Doesn't he know where she's gone?"

"Oh, as I understand it, she left work about a week ago and outside of a dinner party with some bankers and Realtors, she hasn't been seen since. My friend Maggie Lundstrom told me Vivian had had her fill of male admirers, said they expected too much of her, if you know what I mean."

The group moved on and then arrived at the first of the parked cars without another word. One of the women said she'd heard Vivian had been seen with a man no one seemed to know, possibly someone from out of town."

Perfect Imperfection

"Well," said Hope Ziglar, "I hope she knows what she's doing. I met Vivian a couple of times and I rather liked her. She and I are a lot alike. She speaks her mind, if you know what I mean."

"Oh, yes, Hope. We know what you mean," said one of the women with a smile. "We all know what you mean."

The mayor's wife was known to have spoken her mind once or twice too often, much to the chagrin of her husband. It was a constant concern, for he was a politician by nature, but he stood by his wife despite the grief she occasionally caused him.

Chapter 21

Disappeared was perhaps a euphemism for what had happened to Vivian Blaine. None of the women attending the dinner at the Slocum's house knew where she was or what had taken place, of course, but at least two of the men had suspicions that whatever it was, it might not be good. One of them had attended several functions at which Vivian consumed too much alcohol and left the gathering with some man who was not her husband. Several times she had left with two or more men. Ostensibly, they were enjoying each other's company and were going to continue the pleasantries at a local bar. But, thinking back, the gentleman, Pat Tomlinson, also recalled that Vivian had been at Sam's house the night the local lawyers and judges had met there and that Vivian and another young woman had left the party in a big limousine with a couple of lawyers, a Conner's Hill policeman and a newcomer to town named Vincent Sigman.

Still, Tomlinson believed Vivian's disappearance might not be all that serious given her ability to hold her liquor and fend off aggressive admirers. He knew from personal experience that she could hold her own when someone came on too strong. He had made some slight advances toward her himself and discovered rather quickly that she was not to be taken merely as a promiscuous woman. She was after something more than sex or social status. What it was, he was not sure, for she rarely confided in anyone about her feelings, her longings or her ultimate ambitions.

In fact, Tomlinson considered Vivian as somewhat of an enigma. She was coquettish and coy at the same time. She plied her trade, whatever it was, by making men feel as if they were the only ones in whom she had any real interest. She could tell an off-color joke with the best of them, but she could turn into a seemingly demure, unknowing schoolgirl when the occasion called for it. As a result, most of the men with whom she associated found her not only attractive and alluring, but highly intriguing.

Once during an interview that turned into a discussion of local politics and social pretensions, Jesse Stallings had discussed Blaine's enigmatic ways with Tomlinson. "Years ago I dated a girl somewhat like Vivian," the former mayor recalled. "Her name was Grace Miller and she was one of the most interesting females I ever met. In the company of other women she was prim and proper, but with men she was, well… more like a man. Her language was as salty as a sailor's and she could drink beer with the best of them.

"But she was a strange girl. No matter when I called and asked her for a date, she always gave me a straightforward, often blunt answer—a simple 'yes' or 'no'. She never played games like telling me she had a date when she didn't, nor pretended to like something when she didn't. But she never shut me out completely. If she had a date and couldn't go out with me, she told me so, but usually she would say, 'Call me later,' and I usually did. If she wanted to go out, she would say, 'Pick up a six-pack and come on over.'

"She was brought up a Catholic and had strong religious convictions. Nonetheless, on occasions, she was more fanciful and fun-loving that pious. But if you caught her in the wrong mood, she could be testy to say the least. I remember once taking her and a six-pack to a drive-in movie. About thirty minutes into the movie, she and I had both drunk a couple of beers and I reached over to hold her hand and she drew it back as if mine was a pit viper. I knew at once that she was in one of her funky moods, so I didn't try to get any closer to her that night. When I took her home and walked her to the door, I told her I'd had a good time and would call her later. She looked up at me with the most beautiful, blue-green eyes and said, 'Pat, you don't like to make out, do you?'

"Well, what was I supposed to say? I didn't want to annoy her, but I didn't want to tell a lie, so I said, 'Grace, you know me better than that. Of course, I like to make out, but I also know you, and I know that when you get into one of your moods, I'd rather deal with a raging bear.'"

" 'Really. You really like to make out?'

"She said it as solemnly as a prayerful nun."

"Of course, I do," I said.
"You're kidding, aren't you?"
"No, I'm not kidding."
"Okay," she said. "Next time you come over, I'll come tripping down the stairs with a box of condoms between my teeth."

Chapter 22

Jesse Stallings had Tomlinson's description of Grace Miller on his mind as he drove to work the next morning. As he reached the intersection of Main and Mountain streets he noticed the familiar figure of Cee Edmunds plodding along the left side of the street just ahead of him. Edmunds' hulking frame and his movements were unforgettable. He appeared not to walk so much as to fall forward, each step taking him to the edge of an abyss. He found his footing just before plunging headlong into the depths of it.

Looking neither to the right nor left, the brooding Edmunds appeared focused on nothing but empty space. His low brow and broad face belied his intelligence. He had high cheekbones overhanging thick lips. Beneath a round but ample chin his neck, marked by two small vertical scars, sloped at a 45-degree angle backward toward his Adams apple. The scars were a visible remainder of an abnormal growth that had been removed at birth, but the weight of it still seemed to make his head droop.

Edmunds was the son of Charles and Louisa Edmunds. Charles was a civil engineer and Louisa one of two vivacious daughters of George and Irma Bellaire. The Bellaires' ancestry could be traced back to the Revolutionary War when Francoise Bellaire had fought side by side with General Lafayette to help rid the American colonists of their British overlords.

When Cee, the only child of Charles and Louisa, was born he was considered nothing less than a heavenly creature, a star of such luminescence that he would be destined to elevate the Edmunds name to no less than that of his famous forefather. Cee himself was under the spell of no such astronomical illusions. Rather than the foreordained offshoot of some glorious shooting star, he felt himself more the unwitting progeny of an accidental melding of galactic mists. Not only did he abhor the limelight his parents would have for him, he was horrified by the very thought of being a shining example of any sort, heavenly or otherwise. Thus, he became not only a problem student, but the almost silent, enigmatically irrational figure of a man.

The transformation began the day he entered first grade at Conners Hill Elementary School. The name given to him at birth was Charles Edward Edmunds III. He thought the name too long and too stilted and not particularly suited to his personality. He began to call himself C.E. Edmunds, perhaps in imitation of C.V. Simmons, the hawk-nosed, stern looking school principal who commanded respect from students and teachers alike. Moreover, he had decided within a week or two of entering the first grade that there was something magical about the letter 'C', as if it were the simplest way of writing the word "see," the ubiquitous verb of the first-grade primer whose principal characters were Dick and Jane. Later he would come to view the word "see" as the most profound of all English words, as he believed it was the basis of all concrete learning.

All advanced scientific knowledge, he concluded, was based on the observation of physical elements and of their actions and reactions both real and imagined. But mostly it was based on those elements that could be seen in their actual physicality. Seeing was synonymous with knowing, for what could be seen could be known, and knowing was the goal of all learning, or so he believed.

Of course in the primary grades Edmunds could not see the ultimate influence of his early training. Like most children, he first saw only the obvious cause and effect of simple interactions. As he grew older he began to see their hidden effects. Likewise, as he grew into adolescence he became more and more convinced that language, while essential to human conversation, was often an impediment to real learning. His conclusion and its effect antagonized teachers who were more concerned about pedagogical discipline than opening their students eyes to new experiences.

One such incident occurred in a sixth-grade class taught by Miss Prudence Vermeer, a 40-year-old pedagogue who took her education and its attendant responsibilities very seriously. She viewed Cee as having breeched the walls of proper educational etiquette when he failed to answer her roll call one morning.

Perfect Imperfection

Having already observed his presence, Miss Vermeer called his name and received no response. "Charles Edward Edmunds," she called again. Still, no answer. "Would you please stand up, Mr. Edmunds? I can see that you are here, but I can see you better if you are standing."

Cee rose slowly from his seat.

"Why do you not answer to your name, Mr. Edmunds?"

"I prefer 'Cee'," the sixth-grader responded.

"That's all well and good, Mr. Edmunds, but I see from your records that your name is Charles Edmunds. Are you trying to tell me that is not your name, or are you simply trying to disrupt my class?"

"I am not trying to do anything," said Cee. "I am simply stating my preference."

"Do you wish that I record your name simply as C. Edmunds?' she asked.

"I prefer just Cee," he replied.

"Very well, Cee, now will you please answer the roll by saying 'present'."

"Do you not see that I am present?"

"Of course, but I want to know that you will answer the roll correctly in the future?"

"How can you know that if I can only answer 'present' in the present?" he asked.

Somewhat stymied, Ms. Vermeer paused briefly, then continued. "Mr. Edmunds, do you intend to answer 'present' when you are present in the future?"

"I do," said Cee.

"Thank you, Mr. Edmunds."

"I prefer Cee," he repeated.

It was the first but not the last time that Prudence Vermeer would encounter the increasingly recalcitrant streak in Cee Edmunds. Later that year as she began a discussion of geography with her students, she asked the young student how he liked living in Conners Hill.

"Fine," said Cee.

"Fine? Is that it? Just fine? Would you care to elaborate?"

"No."

"Is there any other town you like better than Conners Hill? Some place you had rather be?"

"I prefer to be where I am," Cee answered.

"Is there any place you would like to live or to visit, Mr. Edmunds?"

"It's just Cee," Edmunds replied.

"All right, Cee. Is there any other place you would like to live or to visit?"

"I like to live where I live and to visit where I visit," Cee answered.

"I understand, Cee, but do you not have any travel goals, any aspiration of seeing other parts of the world?"

"No."

"Why not?"

"Because wherever you go, there you are."

"Cee, have you no regard for anything outside of yourself, for any other person, place or thing that is not seen with or through your own eyes? Can you not see that there is something out there that is not dependent upon your own point of view"

"Yes," said Cee.

"Then what would that be?"

"Everything."
"Everything?" Would you care to explain?"
"No."
"Why not?"
"To explain is to take something out of the plain and make it complex!"
"What's wrong with complex?"
"Nothing if you like complex. I prefer plain and simple."
"And what to you is plain and simple, Mr. Edmunds."
"You," Cee replied.

Ms. Vermeer's face turned red and the corners of her mouth changed from a mere sardonic sneer to a glaring scowl.

"Please sit down, Mr. Edmunds," she said, "and this time don't tell me what you prefer!"

Cee Edmunds made it out of the sixth grade but just barely. From then on, most of his teachers felt that he was a precocious, albeit stubborn and incorrigible, student. Few understood his point of view, which in fact had come not from his parents nor his previous teachers but from a single occurrence a few hundred feet from the Conners Hill school.

It came as Cee wandered about the banks of a small creek that ran through the woods bordering the school playgrounds. Teachers sometimes took their students on field trips into the woods to study the local flora and fauna as well as the various types of animals that could be found there. Rabbits and squirrels were numerous, as well as several varieties of birds, butterflies, spiders and praying mantises. For most of the younger boys, the favorite spot was the creek itself. They loved to take off their shoes and wade into it in search of minnows, salamanders and crayfish, all of which were abundant during late spring and early fall. They could be found in the small pools that formed in the bends and twists of the stream that skirted the rocks and broken tree limbs.

On one particularly beautiful day, as Cee waded along the creek in search of crayfish, a small pool in the bend of the stream caught his eye. At first he thought his eyes and his mind were playing tricks on him. The surface of the pool shimmered and moved in swirls of multi-colored patterns as if someone had sprayed the top of it with a very light, oily film. The rays of the sun that penetrated the tree branches above danced on the film causing it to sparkle and shine in some places and to shimmer in others. Instantly, Cee saw something sacred in the shimmering patterns. In some spots they resembled stained-glass windows, in others they defied description, as if they were images traced by the hand of God. He suddenly felt himself lifted above the creek and into a dizzying array of sunlight and clouds high above the forest. Moreover, he felt himself being lifted far above the earth and into a heavenly realm, or what he imagined to be a heavenly realm. Years later he would discover a mystical significance in the seemingly incongruous but symmetrical patterns of a mathematical equation and graphic pattern known as the Mandelbrot Set. It would form the basis of his ultimate hypothesis that the varieties of imperfection in the universe are the foundation of the perfection that God intended. "It is what He got, at least," Edmunds would argue.

Chapter 23

Just outside of town in a wooded area not far from her home, Vivian Blaine lay battered and bruised near a walking trail that circled the town's largest water reservoir. Dried blood from an inch-and-a-half gash in her scalp was matted in her disheveled hair. A large bruise covered her left eye. She tried to raise herself up, but a flash of intense pain shot through her side. It stemmed from two cracked ribs under her left breast. She tried to cry out but was unable to separate her parched, cracked lips enough to utter a sound.

How long she had been there she did not know. Several hours at least, possibly much longer. Lightly clothed, she had been awakened by the chill of the late summer night. A light mist had begun to envelope the usually warm earth and had penetrated her being. Her chest hurt when she breathed. A single thought passed through her mind: I am alive.

She could not recall what had brought her to this place except that she had been enjoying a night on the town. There had been a small party at a local restaurant with several businessmen and their companions, mostly real estate agents and bankers. At dinner the wine was plentiful and the conversation lively.

The man she was with most of the evening was an associate of Sam Slocum, or so she thought. She met him at Sam's the night of the party for the lawyers and judges. He was tall, ruggedly handsome and somewhat quiet, perhaps even shy. She had recalled that before dinner, while most of the guests stood around in Sam's den making small talk, he had been silent, mostly watching and listening, perhaps assessing what each person had to say, perhaps judging each one by the choice of his words, his clothes or his general demeanor. He had said very little. She was fascinated and intrigued and had decided she would find out more about him, who he was and how he came to know Slocum and his wife.

She sauntered up to the stranger, looked into his eyes and said politely, "I don't think we've met, have we, sir? My name is Vivian Blaine. What's yours?"

"Vincent Sigman," said the stranger. "How do you do?"

"I do very well ordinarily," replied Vivian, "but at the moment I'm doing even better."

"And why is that?"

"Because I am talking to you, of course."

"And you consider that doing very well?"

"Well, don't you?"

"I might be persuaded. Are you interested in persuading me?"

"I could be. Do you think that might be arranged?"

"Do you have something in mind?"

"Not at the moment, but I'm sure I could come up with something."

"Fine. Come up with something and let me know what you have in mind and I will let you know if it might be arranged."

That was the extent of the conversation between Vivian and Vincent Sigman on the evening of their first encounter. It was less than a week later that Sigman dropped by the offices of Wolf Johnson and invited Vivian to be his guest at the restaurant dinner party. By then Vivian had learned that Sigman was a New York investment banker as well as a well-heeled real estate developer. His firm, of which he was a major partner, had sent him to Conners Hill to investigate the possibility as to whether Sam Slocum's campaign to create casino gambling in the state was a legitimate one and whether Slocum was a man capable of taking an idea and turning it into a profitable reality.

From the moment Sigman arrived in the small town, he had begun looking into Slocum's business dealings. In addition to being wined and dined by the Realtor and his associates, he had talked with other businessmen and had become convinced that the Conners Hill man was not only capable of organizing a successful campaign, but that he was also capable of turning it into a profitable venture. Indeed, Sigman was already preparing to return to New York with a report recommending that Slocum be extended credit of at least $200 million to get the ball rolling. He had not informed Sam of his intention, but he was on the verge of doing so the night he met Vivian at Sam's party.

Vivian had done a little investigating of her own. She discovered that Vincent's firm, Sigman, Sigman and Bartolomi, was not only a reputable development company but also one with strong ties to several well-known New York political families, as well as to some less than reputable financial families. Using investigative techniques she had learned from her husband, Vivian soon learned that Sigman was a native of New Jersey, was 32 years old, was unmarried but highly sought after by some of New York's most attractive upper-crust socialites. It was enough to whet her most sensual appetites. Therefore when Vincent invited her to the restaurant dinner party, she accepted without reservation. Surely, her husband Ernie would understand that it was merely another step in her plan to become one of the town's most successful women.

Chapter 24

"I'm going out with a group of business friends tonight," Vivian said to Ernie an hour or so before leaving for dinner. "I left some pot roast in the oven for you and the kids. I might be a little late getting home, so don't wait up for me?"

"Where are you going?" asked Sam.

"We're having dinner at the Out West Steak House," Vivian replied. "I'll be there with some businessmen and their wives. It's a social event, but the firm wants me there to take a few notes."

"What kind of notes should your boss want from a social outing?" said Ernie. "I know business and pleasure sometimes mix, but a legal secretary? Who sends a secretary to take notes at a social event? Even Wolf Johnson would be above that sort of thing I would think. The whole thing sounds fishy to me. Are you sure there's not something you're not telling me?"

"Ernie, don't be so suspicious. It's a business thing, nothing more. I'll be home around midnight. Just give the kids their supper and put them to bed by nine o'clock. They have school tomorrow. I'll get them up and give them breakfast. I'll come to bed as soon as I get back."

Ernie knew nothing was ever simple where Vivian was concerned, but at least she was in a good mood. She could be like that most of the time. When she was, she was everything any husband could want in a wife. She was attentive, affectionate, a loving mother, good housekeeper and a sociable partner. And the sex, what there was of it, was always exciting.

The problem was mainly that when Vivian was not in a good mood, she was petulant, irresponsible and downright vindictive. When she drank, which was more and more frequently, she became surly and bitter, as if Ernie was the cause of all her problems as well as her worst enemy, a heavy burden that was dragging her into a life of boredom and regret.

Given her mood on this occasion, Ernie thought little of her evening plans. He expected her to be home when she said she would. He got out the pot roast and sat down with the children to eat. After dinner he told the children to go to their rooms and that they could watch television until bedtime. Once they were settled, he went into the den, turned on the TV and began watching the day's news on CNN. Afterwards he went to the kitchen, poured himself a glass of wine and sat down to watch a rerun of A Face in the Crowd, an old classic movie starring Andy

Perfect Imperfection

Griffith and Patricia Neal. The plot, taken from one of Budd Schulberg's short stories, was one of his favorites. Schulberg could turn out a poignant, thought-provoking story in two or three pages, and although Ernie liked the author's short stories best, he was particularly fond of the his novel, What Makes Sammy Run? He had heard it was based in part on the compulsive obsession of movie producer Mike Todd to overcome his lower class Jewish beginnings on New York's East Side.

Shortly after 11 p.m., when the movie ended, Ernie went to bed. He expected Vivian to let herself in and come to bed soon after midnight so she could be up at dawn to feed the children and get them ready for school. When the sun came up in the morning, however, Ernie found the kids in the kitchen fixing themselves cold cereal and wondering why their mother was not there. Ernie wondered, too, but he didn't think too much of it. Perhaps the milk was gone and she had run to the grocery store to get some. Or maybe she was planning something besides cereal for his own breakfast and had to pick up some eggs or bacon. He went into the den, looked out the window and began to worry. Vivian's Chevy was not in the driveway. Finally it dawned on him. She had been out on the town and had not come home. "Oh, God," he thought, " she's done it again!"

Chapter 25

Vivian Blaine did not show up for work at Wolf Johnson's office at eight o'clock that morning,. No one expected her to be on time, however. Although usually punctual, she could get away with things that few others could, not only because she was efficient and well organized, but because she was beautiful and gracious. Besides being a good secretary, she was a showcase receptionist who greeted everyone who came in the door with a warm smile and a pleasant remark. Johnson himself had once told a legal colleague that "If every business had a Vivian Blaine at the front door, they'd do twice the business they do now." Johnson admitted he often got to work early because Vivian would greet him with a wink and a smile that kept him in a good mood most of the day. Her manner suggested something more than just good natured sociability. She made a man feel as if he were the only one in her life, as if he were the only one for whom she had ever smiled.

Johnson recalled the first time he met her. It was at a Chamber of Commerce business-after-hours function.. At the time she was working as a secretary in Sam Slocum's real estate office. Sam introduced them. Vivian had stared into Johnson's eyes as if they were hypnotic, and Johnson, always a lady's man, responded with reciprocal aplomb. Usually suave and debonair, he was momentarily speechless. Later Slocum confided to the attorney that Vivian wanted to change jobs. He said she wanted something a little more intellectually challenging. "Actually she's an excellent secretary, but it really doesn't matter," said Slocum. "Just look at her. Would you care whether she could type or not?"

Johnson was smitten, and a few weeks later Vivian was his office receptionist. Her wages increased by more than half despite the fact that she had to learn the routine of a legal secretary from the ground up. Her upbringing in the Beeler family, her natural intelligence and her educational background prepared her for most anything she wanted to do. She was a quick study, and despite her insecure childhood and her subsequent misanthropic view of men in general, she could adapt to any business or social situation as if she had been born into it.

At 9 a.m. no one at Johnson and Associates worried why Vivian had not arrived, but at 9:30 several co-workers were beginning to wonder. "It's just not like her," said Bonnie Griffith. "Even when she's been out late in the evening she's usually here by nine fifteen. Or she's called in if something has come up. It isn't like her to be late without letting us know."

Just then the phone on Vivian's desk rang. Bonnie answered it. "Johnson and Associates," she said. "May I help you....? Oh, Mr. Blaine, we were just talking about Vivian and wondering if she's all right this morning. She's usually here by now....No, we don't know where she is. We were hoping you could tell us."

Bonnie put her hand over the telephone mouthpiece and whispered to the other two secretaries. "It's Ernie Blaine. He says Vivian didn't come home last night and he's worried about her. He wants to know if we know where she might be." The other women opened their arms, held their palms up and looked at the ceiling as if to say, "Who knows?"

"I'm sorry, Mr. Blaine, but no one at the office has the slightest idea where she might be. I thought perhaps one of the children was sick or something and she had to go to the doctor. Her car isn't there? Don't worry, I'm sure she'll turn up soon. Vivian can take care of herself. It's probably just a matter of time before she gets home. If she comes straight to the office instead, we'll let you know."

Bonnie hung up the phone. "Go tell Wolf what's going on. He'll want to know." She hadn't seen Johnson as he stepped into the front office behind her.

"What do you need to tell me?" he asked.

"Wolf, that was Ernie Blaine on the phone. He said Vivian didn't come home last night. Or at least, if she came home, she went back out. Her car's gone and he's worried to death. He mentioned something about her going out to do some work for the firm last night and wondered if you might have any idea where she went afterward."

"Thanks,. I'll take care of it. Bonnie, fill in for Vivian at the front desk today and we'll find out where she is and see if we can't straighten this out."

"Certainly, Mr. Johnson. I hope nothing serious has happened to Vivian. "

"Don't worry. I'll take care of it," Wolf repeated.

Chapter 26

Wolf Johnson walked back to the dimly lit office buried in the bowels of the two-story brick building that once had been the home away from home of a revered pharmacist and the back room of the Conners Hill Democratic political machine. Now it was a cave filled with memorabilia of all sorts, from black Indian elephants and antique beer mugs to a modern day barometer and the weather-beaten, worm-holed wheel of an old sailing ship. Most of the relics were things Johnson had brought back from trips throughout the world. They were the stuff of a man for whom trophies of all sorts were a measure of a man's success and importance. They were an indication that he had been places and seen things that other men had not. They were proof that a small town boy could take his place among the big-time players of the world. But even more than that, they brought back vivid memories of youth and adventure, of visions realized, dreams fulfilled, of long lost loves regained. If the rest of one's life was trivial and mundane, a good part of it had been exciting and glorious.

These were not Johnson's thoughts as he returned to the cave however, for although he was fond of visiting the past, he was not one to live there. The world existed here and now and he was more at home in the real world than in past illusions. As soon as he reached his somewhat cluttered desk, he picked up the phone and dialed Sam Slocum's number. It buzzed several times before Sam answered. It was several seconds before he spoke.

"Good morning. This is Sam. What's on your mind?"

"Sam, Wolf Johnson here. I've got a little problem and thought you might help."

"What's the problem, Wolf. Someone not living up to expectations? You know how it goes. You give a little, you get a little."

"Cut the crap, Sam. You know me. I usually get what I want, but that's not the point. I sent Vivian out last night to do a little background research for me and she's not back yet. She hasn't come to work this morning. Ernie called and said she didn't come home last night. You were at that dinner party, weren't you? Who did she leave the party with?"

"Actually, I wasn't there, Wolf. Judith and I had another engagement and couldn't get out of it. Besides I understand it was mostly bankers. You know I'm not one of those. But hold on a minute, Sandy Smythe is here. She goes out with James Earl and I think he was there. Maybe she knows."

Slocum took the phone away from his ear and Johnson could hear him and Sandy talking in the background: "You know who she was with, Sandy?"

"Well, I don't think she came with anyone, but she was being awful chummy with that new guy in town. What's his name? Winston? Benton? Oh, yeah, Vincent, Vincent something or other."

"Vincent Sigman? The guy from New York?" asked Sam.

"Yeah, that's it. Got a Yankee accent but real good looking. I'd go out with him any time."

"Yeah, we know that, honey, but he's not your type. He's got brains as well as brawn."

Sam put the phone back to his ear. "You hear that, Wolf? Sandy doesn't know who Vivian left with, but she was with Vincent Sigman, my associate from New York. I wouldn't worry too much about that. Vincent's a straight arrow kind of guy. All business, if you know what I mean. He's not about to jeopardize our business arrangement with some fly-by-night hanky-panky. Besides, he could have any dame in New York if he wanted her."

Johnson paused for a moment. "Sam, Vivian's a special kind of woman, and I'm not trying to pry into her personal life. I'm just worried about the fact that nobody knows where she is this morning. Maybe I'm a little too anxious, but she's a helluva good secretary and this office would be a different place without her."

"Well, Wolf, I'll make a few calls and see what I can find out. Maybe some of the guys I know can tell us where she is. I'll check around and call you back as soon as I find out."

"I appreciate it, Sam. Maybe somebody knows what happened to her."

Chapter 27

Around seven o'clock that evening Cee Edmunds was finishing his stroll along the banks of the Conners Hill lake. He enjoyed walking in the late afternoon as the sun began to set near the farthest end of the reservoir. The golden glow of its warm rays shimmered on the surface like a myriad blinking stars. Today, only the wake of a small rowboat broke the mesmerizing tranquility of the glittering water as a lone fisherman headed back to the dock. No one else was in sight as Edmunds turned up the narrow path that led to his cottage near the top of the hill. Hardly anyone else ever used the path or even knew about it. It was his own private walk from the back of his property to the lake. Not even the county's park attendants knew it was there or where it went. Occasionally an adventuresome youth would begin the trek up the hill but turn back when it appeared that the path was more illusory than real. It was an illusion that gave Edmunds the privacy he preferred.

Cee was somewhat lost in his thoughts. He had appeared in district court that morning to defend himself against several charges, including one of assaulting a police officer. The charge had arisen from one of his late night strolls through downtown Conners Hill. A harmless incident, it began as a mere traffic stop but took an unexpected turn when the policeman attempted to take him in for resisting arrest.

Cee was lucky. His case was the first one on the docket and, as fortune would have it, Abraham Lincoln Sherf was the presiding judge. The bailiff had already called the court to order and Sherf had arranged his files, straightened his silver-rimmed glasses and ordered one Charles Edward Edmunds to rise and enter his plea of guilty or not guilty.

"How do you plead, Mr. Edmunds?" the judge inquired.

"Not guilty, your Honor."

"Mr. Heath, what is the nature of the charges against Mr. Edmunds?" Judge Sherf asked of the assistant district attorney.

"He was jay-walking, resisting arrest and assaulting a police officer, your honor."

Judge Sherf looked at Cee, noticed a slight grin on his face and knew he was trouble. He had heard of Edmunds' eccentricities from Magistrate Irma Robrock before court that morning and he was expecting something unusual. It came sooner than he expected.

"Tell us what happened, Officer Vanhoy," Sherf said to the arresting officer.

"Well, your Honor. I was making a routine check of some of the downtown businesses a little past midnight when I spotted Mr. Edmunds here walking down the middle of Main Street. He was holding out his arms and sort of wavering from side to side as if he was pretending to be an airplane. I figured he was inebriated and needed to go home and sleep it off, so I went up to him and asked him what he was doing. He didn't say anything but kept on walking, so I told him to halt, which he did. I asked him if he had been drinking and he said no, but I didn't believe him."

"Did you smell any alcohol on him?" Judge Sherf asked.

"No, your Honor, but he reeked of something."

"Do you know what it was?"

"No, sir. It might have been turpentine or paint thinner. It sure wasn't no aftershave though."

"How do you know?"

"It was too strong. No man in his right mind would wear that kind of lotion."

"Very well, go on," Sherf said.

"He was walking in the middle of the street and I asked him to move to the sidewalk as he was endangering himself and the motoring public, but he refused. He said it was a public highway and he was a member of the public. I told him the street was for vehicular traffic, not pedestrians, and that if he didn't move to the sidewalk I would arrest him for jaywalking."

"What did he say to that?"

"He said jaywalking was crossing a street against a stoplight, not walking down the middle of it. I asked him if he wanted me to charge him with resisting arrest, and he said he wasn't resisting, he was just making a point. I told

Perfect Imperfection

him to put his hands behind his back in order to 'cuff him. I took hold of his left wrist to put it behind his back and he butted me in the face with his head. At that point I slung him to the ground, handcuffed him and took him to the station."

"Is that all?"

"Yes, sir."

"Mr. Edmunds, what do you have to say for yourself?"

Cee stood silent, as if he had not heard the judge's question.

"Mr. Edmunds, please give me your account of what happened, otherwise I shall have to send you back to jail immediately."

Cee raised his head and stared into Sherf's eyes.

"I was going home, your Honor. I was walking the line."

"What line is that, Mr. Edmunds?"

"The white line."

"You were walking down the center line of Main Street headed toward home? Is that right?"

"Yes, your Honor."

"Where is home, Mr. Edmunds?"

"Where I live."

"How do you get there.?

"I take the white line to the railroad, turn left and walk the railroad line to the metal recycling plant, turn right and take a beeline through the woods."

"Why did you butt this officer in the face with your head?"

"When he grabbed my arm, he dropped his walkie-talkie. We both bent over to pick it up and we bumped heads. I didn't mean to butt him."

Judge Sherf smiled a knowing smile and spoke curtly to the arresting officer. "Mr. Vanhoy, is that what happened?"

"It might be, your Honor?"

"Officer Vanhoy, either it is or it isn't. Which is it?"

"Well, it could have been it."

"Officer, did Mr. Edmunds here curse you or make any other threatening gesture that would lead you to believe he intended to do you harm?"

"No, your Honor, except that he was not cooperative. He refused to move to the sidewalk."

"Were there any cars or other vehicles coming down the street at the time?

"I don't think so, your Honor."

"Mr. Edmunds, how long have you lived in Conners' Hill?"

"Fifty-two years."

"Have you ever been arrested for resisting arrest, assault or jaywalking before?"

"No, your Honor. "

"Will you commit any of these offenses in the future?"

"I don't know, sir. I can't predict the future."

"Let me rephrase the question. Do you plan to commit any of these offenses in the future?"

"No, sir."

"Very well, Mr. Edmunds. I find you not guilty of the charges of jaywalking, resisting arrest or assaulting an officer. However, I believe you owe Officer Vanhoy here an apology for creating a situation that could possibly have ended with some serious consequences. Are you willing to apologize to this officer for creating that situation?"

"I am, your Honor."

"Then do it now."

Cee Edmunds turned to the police officer and said: "Officer Vanhoy. I apologize for my behavior and yours."

As far as Edmunds was concerned, the incident was over and nothing had occurred." His thoughts later that day were not of what happened, but of what has happening now: the beautiful sunset, the sparkling water, the lush green leaves of the trees.

Moments later Cee heard the moans and saw the limp body of Vivian Blaine lying just a few feet from his path through the woods.

Chapter 28

The sun was setting as Cee bent over Vivian Blaine to see what injuries she might have. His first thought was to go for help, but he knew the lake park would be closing in a few minutes and there would be no one else who might find her before night fell and the sounds of the forest muffled her own. She moaned as Cee picked her up and began the climb toward the top of the hill and his cottage. Several minutes later, the light faded and Cee plodded onward in near darkness. With Vivian still in his arms, he reached the back door of the small cottage and entered the kitchen. He turned on the light and glanced down at her face. Beneath the blood and the matted hair, he saw that the young woman in his arms was as beautiful as anyone he had ever seen. He carried her down a small hallway to his only bedroom and laid her gently on the bed. The corners of her mouth curled upward slightly and she tried to speak.

"Thank..., thank..."

"Be still," said Cee. "I'll be back in a moment." He went back into the hall, opened a small door and grabbed a towel from a neatly folded stack. He returned to the kitchen, turned on the hot water spigot and let the water run a few minutes before wetting the towel. He opened a small cabinet beside the kitchen window, took out a glass and filled it with warm water. He opened another cabinet door and took out a small bowl of sugar. He put several tablespoons of sugar into the glass of warm water, stirred it vigorously, put it to his lips to see if it was not too warm, and then returned to the bedroom.

"Here, drink what you can of this," Cee said to Vivian as he bent over her with the glass. She smiled faintly. He lifted her head and she sipped the liquid slowly at first, then opened her mouth and drank hungrily from the glass. Cee lowered her head back onto the pillow. Vivian closed her eyes and breathed slowly. Cee took the wet towel and began to wipe the blood and hair from her forehead. "What happened?" she said.

"You must have fallen," said Cee. "You've got some pretty bad bruises."

"I don't remember."

"That may be best," said Cee, "but it'll come back in time. It always does."

Vivian smiled as if in agreement, then she closed her eyes and drifted off into sleep. Cee put a light blanket over her before going back to the kitchen to get himself a drink of water. With glass in hand he walked back to the front room of the cottage. He sat down in a large chair, picked up a book from a table beside the chair and began to read from a poem by Joe Bruno.

> Invincible youth you take it too far,
> Take risks and wish on a burned out star.
> You think everything is just like TV,
> "Nothin' ever gonna happen to me."

What is it that we take too far? thought Cee. Is it simply our innate optimism, our unquestioning belief, our trust that life will turn out for the best? Or is it merely a blind acceptance of our ignorance, an ignorance that has us assume we are invincible? After all, things do happen. Good and bad, they happen. Our pain comes from judging them as good or bad, not just as things that happen.

He read on.

> It takes one more step and you find the end,
> It might be you, or it might be your friend.
> Step back a minute and you see the truth:
> The world lost one more invincible youth.

Is this woman just one more lost youth, or is she something more sinister than that? thought Cee. Did she merely fall, or was she pushed? Did she merely succumb to gravity or did she push someone who pushed her back?

He believed he knew the answer. He had discovered it years ago. It was the randomness of the universe. It was a perfect imperfection. Without it, life would be bland and boring, totally predetermined, totally organized, totally disciplined, totally colorless. God had intended it to be chaotic, disorganized, disorderly. Distinct and distasteful at times, yes, but always filled with color and wonder, always frantic and fanciful, fearful and fun. Like a ride on a great roller-coaster. Up and down, around and around, mournful and mind-boggling but never boring.

Cee Edmunds had pondered the universe and had accepted its dictates. It was what it was. To have it be otherwise was to row one's boat upstream, not downstream. It was to go against the tide, to sail into the wind, to cast one's lot with sinners. It was to deny God by defying God.

Edmunds realized that soon someone would be looking for the blond-haired beauty who had stumbled into his arms. And they would be looking to blame someone for what had happened to her. Regardless of what was said of Vivian, someone would blame him for having found her, for having revived her, for having put her on the road to recovery. In time, she would give them good reason.

Chapter 29

Six days later, in the offices of downtown Conners Hill, the word was out that Vivian Blaine, the wayward wife of Ernie Blaine, was missing. No one had seen nor heard from her in the past week. She had disappeared without a trace.

There was some talk that Ernie might have done her in, that he had become fed up and couldn't take it any more. After all, despite her beauty and her brains, Vivian was an unfaithful wife. She was no better than a common slut, a woman who gave herself to any man who smiled and hinted that he could open the door to a bigger office, a better title, a greater degree of personal power. From all appearances, that was the case. But behind the appearance, Vivian's story was somewhat more complicated. Money and power were not her goals. She had come from money and she had neither love nor respect for it. Her father had lavished her with money and things, with jewelry, clothes and expensive cars. His actions had proven to her that money was nothing more than a facade, a symbol of power behind which often lay little more than greed and gluttony, In her mind, real power was the ability to deny those things, to stand up to hypocrisy, to destroy deceit, to annihilate false images. Real power was the strength and ability to defy the illusions of grandeur exhibited by the world's power-mongers, to annihilate the idiotic ideology of self-inflated politicians and matinée idols, to see the world as it is, not as they wished it to be.

The irony was that few people in Conners Hill saw Vivian as anything other than a beautiful blonde. It was an image she actively cultivated. She wanted everyone to believe she was exactly what she appeared to be, especially the high and mighty men of wealth. She understood that when everything is judged by its image, image becomes the standard of reality. As long as it looks good, it is good. If it looks like a dog, it is a dog. Vivian had learned from first-hand experience that such was not the case, but she had been taking great pains to prove otherwise.

"I knew from the first time I ever met her that Vivian would come to no good," said Nan Seemore, a shop owner, to several of her friends during lunch at The Coffee Spoon, a popular downtown cafe. "Several of us were having a snack here one day and we were casually talking about our husbands and our families when Vivian spoke up and said, 'I'm happily married—until I meet a handsome man.' Well, what do you think? We all sort of sat there with our mouths open. We were stunned."

"She was kidding, of course. Wasn't she?" said Bebe Bullis. "I mean, we've all met her. We know she likes to kid. She didn't really mean that, did she? And even if she did, she didn't mean she would do anything about it? I mean she didn't say anything more than we all think sometimes. Really, how many of us haven't had our heads turned by a handsome man?"

"Bebe, it's one thing to have your head turned. It's another thing to turn your marriage into a sham. No, I'm afraid Vivian is a member of the wham-bam-thank-you-mam generation. She's a slut and that's all there is to it."

"Well, I feel sorry for her." said Bullis. "She obviously doesn't know what she's doing. Nobody with any common sense would put a husband, even a bad one, through a ringer like that and come out on top. And think of what it's doing to the children. They may be little, but they know a lot more than we give them credit for. No doubt they'll turn out as mixed up and confused as Vivian."

Janice Stallings listened to the conversation and wondered what Vivian would have said had she been there. She and Jesse had heard of Vivian's disappearance the night they were leaving the Slocums. She had spoken with Jesse about it when they returned home and he had brushed off the news as if it were nothing.

"People don't just disappear," Jesse had said. "If they do, they disappear to somewhere. They don't just fall off the face of the earth. Vivian will show up somewhere and all the talk about her will be just that—talk. If women didn't have something to talk about, they wouldn't know what to do with themselves. That's why men go to work. They want to do something besides talk."

"But Jesse," Janice had interjected, "what if something really bad has happened to Vivian. What if she's been beaten or killed? What would Ernie and the children do?"

"What if," Jesse replied. "That's a big word—if. In fact it may be the most abused word in the English language. Back when I was young and I used that phrase, my father would say to me, 'If a bullfrog had wings, he wouldn't bump his ass so much'."

"But Jesse, aren't the 'what ifs' the basis of all our military and political analysis and planning? Aren't 'what ifs' part of the creative process by which we envision all the possibilities and consequences of our intended actions. If we didn't use any 'what ifs', we would be likely to make some serious mistakes."

"I'll grant you that, but too often we take the 'what ifs' as if they were the real thing and then miss the real things. For instance, all the what ifs about Vivian Blaine are based more on idle speculation than appraisal of the facts. We need to assess the facts and determine what we know and then proceed with the what ifs. For instance, what do we really know about Vivian Blaine's so-called disappearance? First of all, we know that she hasn't been seen or heard from in several days, maybe a week. Does that mean she has disappeared or merely that nobody has seen or heard from her? Second, we know from Wolf Johnson that Vivian didn't go to work this week and that Ernie doesn't know where she is. Does that mean she has disappeared? Not necessarily. Perhaps she's been in an accident and has amnesia. Or perhaps she simply decided to skip town for a while, to get away from all the speculation and gossip about her? Or, maybe, just maybe, she's simply playing hard to find because it keeps her at the center of attention. You know, some people will go to extremes to prove they are indispensable to other people. Maybe she's just trying to prove to Ernie that he loves her and would be lost without her."

"Jesse, sometimes you are just plain impossible. Aren't your scenarios just as speculative as mine? Aren't you just saying: what if she's not lost, what if she's just hiding out? But what if she's not? What if she's been killed or kidnapped? Don't we need to look for her? After all, as bad as she may be, she's still a human being and worthy of our concern."

"Jan, you are right, of course. I'll see what I can find out. I'll call Wolf, see what he knows and then check with Chief Grady. Perhaps he'll have heard something in case there's any foul play involved. In the meantime, you check with anybody you know who might be close to Vivian. Maybe they already know where she is."

Chapter 30

Inside the office of Sam Slocum a heated debate was raging.

"What the hell is going on here, Vincent? You say you ate with Vivian at the meeting and you offered to take her home but she refused? Why don't I believe that? Why would she refuse you? She doesn't refuse anybody as far as I know."

"Why would you say that, Sam? I find Vivian a very attractive woman, but after all, she is married. She's got a head on her shoulders and I can't believe she would get involved in any way with someone she doesn't really know. Yeah, I admit she's flirtatious, but that isn't a sin, is it? From what I understand maybe she's flirtatious to a fault, but I can't really believe she's a bad person. How many of us haven't made a mistake or two in our lives?"

"Believe me, Vincent, Vivian has made enough mistakes for a lifetime. I mean she went to work for me didn't she? She knew I hired her more for her looks and personality than for anything she knew about the real estate business. She saw me as a way out of an ordinary, routine life and she took it. And she was good at it, if you know what I mean."

Vincent looked puzzled. He didn't know what Sam meant but he could guess. It hadn't taken him long to learn that Sam was something of a womanizer. Just for clarification he started to ask Sam what he meant, then thought better of it and kept it to himself. If Vivian was somehow less than the person he had come to know through their few casual meetings, he did not want to know it. He wanted to see her more as a kind of blond goddess—well, maybe not a goddess, but at least as a woman a cut above the women he was used to attracting. He imagined her as much more than the New York socialites who wanted only to look good and enjoy life without worries or cares. His instinct told him that Vivian was much more than that, that she was searching for a life of purpose and meaning but thus far had not found it.

Most good women, Vincent believed, discovered value simply in being who they were and in the promises of marriage, motherhood and taking care of one's self and of others. Sure, there were some for whom the simple life was not enough, those who had to taste the so-called 'finer things in life' in order to believe their lives were meaningful. They wanted beautiful homes, fine cars, expensive jewelry and husbands who catered to their every wish. He thought such women believed themselves to be better than others and more deserving but in the end were merely trying to be someone they were not. They were trying to be more than ordinary human beings. They failed to realize that ordinary human beings are those that make the world work. Perhaps Vivian Blaine wanted to become an ordinary human being but was one whose upbringing stood in the way.

"Well, Vincent," Sam said. "Do you have any idea who left the restaurant with Vivian that night? She had to have some way to get home."

"I thought she drove herself," Vincent said. "In fact, she said to me that she was going straight home because she had to get to bed and get her kids ready for school in the morning. I followed her out and waved goodbye when she left."

"Where was she going when you waved goodbye?"

"She had started through the parking lot at the restaurant. I assumed she was going to her car, and I simply turned around and went back into the building. I didn't actually see her get into her car. Perhaps someone was waiting for her."

"No doubt."

"You have any idea who it might have been?"

"Not a clue."

"You think it was the one who brought her to the restaurant, someone who picked her up at home?

"Not really because she left home in her car."

Maybe it was one of the female Realtors who attended the dinner and left just before Vivian left. That's possible, isn't it?

"Sure, any thing's possible, but what do we have to go on? Did you notice any of the people there who left early?"

"Not that I can remember. I didn't know half the people there, and I wouldn't have paid much attention to who left early or who didn't. It could have been anybody."

"Is there anything that you can remember that might give us a clue, anything that might have indicated where she was going when she left?"

"Not that I recall...Oh, wait a minute...At one point in our dinner conversation, Vivian said she had to make a phone call. She was gone for about five minutes and when she came back she said she had called Ernie to check on the kids and that he had asked her to pick up some beer on the way home."

Sam looked puzzled. "That's odd. I know a little about Ernie Blaine and he's a kind of a weird fellow in a way. I don't think he drinks beer. Told me once that beer is for people with no real sense of taste. Said he only drinks wine. 'The fruit of the vine is the nectar of the Gods,' he said. I remember saying that most of us think real men drink beer, that only wimps drink wine. He said real men drink anything they want to, even wine. He said real men drink what they like, not what other people think they should like."

"So you don't think Ernie would have asked Vivian to buy beer for him?"

"No, but somebody else might."

"Oh, great. We've narrowed down our search to all the men who like beer. Got any other ideas?"

"Not at the moment. How about you?"

"Maybe we could ask some of the other guys at the dinner if they remember anyone besides Vivian leaving early. Kingston Armour was one of the Realtors there, maybe he knows."

Vincent waited while Sam picked up the phone and dialed Armour's number. In a moment he answered.

"King, Sam Slocum here. You were at the bankers' dinner the other night, weren't you? Do you remember if any one of the women there left the dinner early, or at least shortly after the meal was over? Vincent and I were trying to figure out if Vivian Blaine left with any of the other women?"

Another moment passed. "You don't remember any other woman leaving the group early? You didn't happen to hear Vivian mention who she was leaving with, did you? Her disappearance has got us stumped and we're trying to figure out what happened?"

After another short pause, Slocum hung up the phone. "Kingston doesn't have any idea whether anyone else left the party early. He doesn't think they did."

Chapter 31

The following morning Jesse Stallings was awakened by a strange dream. He dreamed he had seen his mother and grandmother in an embassy building in Washington, D.C. They were attending some sort of reception and Jesse was perplexed by the dream. Later, as he drove into town, he saw the figure of Cee Edmunds as Edmunds plodded along the sidewalk headed toward the town's main intersection. He pulled over to the curb, rolled down his window and called to the hulking figure on the sidewalk.

"Cee, where are you going this morning?"

Edmunds pointed to his mouth but said nothing.

"Breakfast? Are you going to Charlie's for breakfast?"

Edmunds nodded.

"Mind if I join you?"

Edmunds shook his head.

"Okay. I'll park in the back and meet you inside."

Perfect Imperfection

Charlie's sandwich shop was a favorite hangout for old-timers in Conners Hill. Built in what once had been a 10-foot wide alley between two downtown stores, it consisted mostly of a single room that filled the former space. In the middle of the room a counter ran parallel with the walls. On one side of the counter against the wall on the right were a grill, refrigeration units, preparation counters and utensils. On the other side was a row of short, red, round-top stools and just enough room for new arrivals to pass by on their way to the four booths in the back of the building. Behind the booths there was a short hallway and two small restrooms. Beyond them was the back door. Cee entered the building from the front. Finding all the stools occupied, he headed for the back booths. Jesse entered the restaurant from the back door and sat down in a booth. Cee slid into a seat opposite him. He had a copy of the Selwin Daily Mirror in his hand.

"Anything worth reading in the paper this morning?" Jesse inquired.

Cee shook his head.

"Hasn't been anything there about the whereabouts of Vivian Blaine has there?"

Cee appeared a little fidgety at the mention of Vivian's name, but he didn't say anything. He raised his empty palms as if to say he didn't know anything about her disappearance. Jesse noticed that his brow wrinkled slightly.

Jesse had known Cee most of his life and wondered why he had felt an impulse to join Edmunds for breakfast. The younger man was hardly a conversationalist, but he was a good listener. For some reason Jesse felt he could open up to Cee and know that whatever he said, it would not be repeated. He hardly ever repeated anything.

"I had a crazy dream last night, Cee. I thought you might help me decipher it."

Edmunds raised his palms again.

"I dreamed I was in an embassy building in Washington, D.C. and my mother and grandmother were there. There appeared to be some kind of reception going on and we were all in a line heading down a long corridor. My mother was standing in front of me and my grandmother arrived a little later all dressed up as if she was going to church or something. When grandmother first walked up to me, I said to her, 'Grandmother, you can't be here because you're dead. My mom turned around and said, 'No, son. I see her too. She's real.'

"'But Mom, you're dead, too,' I replied. 'The man behind me in the line was an old friend from college. He nodded as if to say what was happening was real."

Cee seemed unconcerned. Finally, he spoke.

"Why an embassy building?" he asked.

"'I don't know. Perhaps because years ago when I was in the Marine Corps, I was stationed at Quantico, Virginia and used to go into Washington on the weekends. Every now and then I drove along embassy row. Also, over the building entrance, there was some kind of foreign inscription.'"

"What kind of inscription?"

"I don't know. Just foreign."

"What was the reception for?"

"I don't know that either. It just looked as if we were all waiting for something to happen, and we had to stand in line to wait."

"Any attaché cases?"

"Not that I noticed."

"What language?"

"What?"

"The inscription. What language was it?"

Jesse hesitated.

"I don't know."

Suddenly an image appeared in Jesse's head. He nearly choked on the coffee he had just swallowed. Tears welled up in his eyes and he could not speak.

"Oh, my God."

"What?"

"I ...I know what the dream was about?"

"What?"

"The inscription over the entrance. It was Greek."

"So?"

"It wasn't an embassy building. It was the student union building at Duke. It was the day of my graduation." Jesse choked on his words again.

"And..."

"I wasn't there."

Cee looked perplexed.

"Why not?" he said.

"I had a history paper to write."

"So?"

"In Charleston, South Carolina."

"Charleston?"

"The title of my paper was 'The Lyceum Movement in Charleston, S.C, 1825 to 1850'."

"And?"

"It was a graduate history course. I had to pass it to graduate."

"And?"

"I hadn't been able to find any material on it in Durham or Chapel Hill before the semester ended. I went to Charleston to find the material. I was there on the day of my graduation."

"And?"

"My mother and grandmother put me through college. They couldn't be there when I graduated because I wasn't there. I came home from Charleston, wrote a 50-page paper in three days and took it to Durham. My professor had given me an incomplete grade and a week to finish the paper. I took it to him and he sent me a postcard the next day saying I had passed the course. I got my diploma three months later."

"And the dream?"

"It was my graduation and my mother and grandmother were there!"

Jesse thanked Cee for his help.

"You're welcome," Edmunds said.

Just before the two men left Charlie's, Stallings said, "You know, Cee, I've had nightmares about my difficulties in college for thirty years or more. Now, I think they're over."

"Good," said Cee.

As Jesse walked away from the reclusive Edmunds a thought occurred to him. It was that he had chosen a career as a newspaper reporter and editor, a career in which his primary function had been to turn papers in on time day after day. He had performed the penance for 30 years.

Then another thought crossed his mind. He wondered if he would have ever understood the dream without Cee's simple questions. Could the meaning of life be grasped as simply? He wondered.

Chapter 32

Later that day the Conners Hill News editor asked himself another question. Could a woman simply disappear without a trace? He thought not, but so far Vivian had managed to pull it off. How?

Jesse talked to Sam after the latter's conversation with Vincent Sigman. He learned that Vivian had walked out of the restaurant and into the parking lot where there were lots of cars. If she had not been going to her own car, whose was she going to? If anyone had seen her, how would he go about finding them?

He decided to call Dave Devlin. He would ask Dave if he had ever tracked down anyone who was there one minute and gone the next. If so, how did he find them?

Jesse picked up the phone and dialed Devlin's number. Dave answered on the second buzz.

"Devlin Investigative Services, may I help you?

"Dave, this is Jesse Stallings. I've run into a little problem and need some help. Could you spare a few minutes to let me pick your brain."

"Sure, Jesse. Mary and I were just on our way into town to pick up some printing supplies. Mary can shop while you and I talk."

"That's great, Dave. I'd really appreciate it. How long do you think it will take you to get here?"

"We're about halfway there now. I'd say not more than five minutes or so. Shall I just come on up when I get there?"

"Yeah. I'll meet you in the conference room."

Devlin arrived at the News office exactly five minutes after Jesse hung up. His face was alight with the Irish pixie grin that seemed a permanent fixture. It was a smile as disarming as any Jesse had ever seen. It made perfect strangers feel as if they were long-lost friends.

"How've ya been, Jesse? Put any money into the casino business yet?"

"I'm still assessing the situation, as they say in movies. Haven't decided whether you'd call money in the casino business an investment or a gamble. I'm not much of a gambler. If I had been, I'd have started my own newspaper a long time ago."

Devlin nodded his approval. Gambling was not his choice of addiction either. He'd seen too many gamblers ride their luck right into the poorhouse. He wanted no part of it."

"So what's on your mind, Jesse. What's the problem you mentioned on the phone?

"Well, strictly speaking, it isn't my problem. And the fact is I don't know if it's anybody's problem, except maybe Ernie Blaine's."

"Yeah, what about Ernie? Anything happen to him?"

"I thought you'd probably heard by now. His wife, Vivian, has been missing for nearly a week. Seems she disappeared out of the parking lot at Out West Steakhouse and hasn't been heard from since. A lot of local people are concerned that something bad might have happened to her."

"Vivian Blaine. I'm not sure I know who you're talking about. But keep talking, she sounds intriguing. I've dealt with a lot of women in parking lots. Some good, some bad, some not so hot."

"Vivian is the tall blonde who has been working in Wolf Johnson's office for about six months. She's anything but a dumb blonde. Besides being extremely attractive, she has a head on her shoulders. The question is whether or not she's using it for good or ill."

"Oh, okay Jesse, now I know who you're talking about. I've seen her a couple of times in Johnson's office. She's not just good looking, she's a knockout. Be hard for her to stay missing long. Oh, and come to think of it, I've seen her once before."

"When was that?"

"The night I tailed Alan Malloy out to the party for the lawyers and judges at Sam Slocum's. I think she was one of the party people."

"That figures."

"How so?"

"From what I've learned about Vivian, she has something more up her sleeve than just partying. I'm afraid there's something about her that's more sinister than that."

"Got any idea what it might be?"

"Not really. It's more a hunch than anything else, but I've learned to play my hunches over the years. More often than not, they led me to a good story. You can mark my words, Vivian Blaine is more than a mere wayward wife. I just haven't figured out what."

"Jeez, Jesse, no wonder you stayed in this business so long. You really get your kicks out of it, don't you?"

"Well, don't you?"

"What do you men?"

"What I mean is: we both like a good mystery. More than that we like trying to solve them. It's a game of sorts, kind of like crossword puzzles or chess. Only we're playing with real people, not words or pawns."

"Why do you think we like games? They can be a waste of time."

"Isn't life a kind of game? It begins, we play, it ends. The object is not so much whether we win or not, because we all know we can't win. The game will end and we'll be out of it. We can only hope there's another game."

"I thought the object of playing a game was to win it."

"Not really. Maybe the only object of a game is to play it with all our attention, to spend time without thinking and worrying too much. How many football or baseball players are thinking about how they are playing when they're playing. Not many, I would guess. They're just playing. That's the beauty of good physical games, being active without thinking too much."

"Yeah, Jesse, but our kind of games require a lot of thinking and not much action. Thinking is the action in bridge, chess or crossword puzzle-solving."

"You've got a point there, Dave. But in those games the focus is still on doing something with our full attention. Thinking about how to solve a problem can drive out thinking about other things. Works out pretty much the same as physical sports, doesn't it?"

"I guess so. So, now that we've solved that, how should we go about finding Vivian or how she disappeared?"

"You said she left the steakhouse and went into the parking lot and that's the last we know about her, right?"

"Yeah."

"So how do we find out who was in the parking lot?"

"That's what I called you for, Dave. I thought maybe you might know how."

"Okay, let's begin by checking the parking lot. If Vivian left the restaurant with someone else, maybe her car's still in the lot. If that's the case, we need to check on who was in the restaurant that night that might have seen her leave or might have seen her leave with someone."

"We already know a little because we know who was in her group at dinner. Sam's already talked to most of them, including Vincent Sigman, who sat with her during the meal. But Sam's talked to everyone else. Nobody seems to remember when she left or with whom."

"Maybe she left with someone who wasn't in the group, maybe someone who was eating at the restaurant but wasn't a part of the group. That's a possibility isn't it?"

"Well, sure, Dave. But where does that leave us?"

"Pretty much back at square one, but square one isn't a dead end necessarily. We need to find out if there were any other groups there that night or if the wait staff remembers any particular individuals who were there. And for that matter, maybe one of the waiters or waitresses remembers Vivian and somebody she might have left with. As good looking as Vivian is, I'm sure a waiter or two took note of her. Maybe one of them knows her personally. It's worth asking at the very least."

Stallings liked the way Dave's mind worked. Maybe it was like that for most private detectives. They seemed always open to possibilities. "Never assume the door is the only way out of the building," Dave would say. "When you get in a jam, you may have to make your own door." The PI's fictional detective Harry Paine often made his own door, otherwise he wouldn't have survived.

Dave said he would stop by the restaurant on his way home and ask around. Maybe something would turn up. In the meantime he suggested that Jesse call Sam and ask him to find out if anyone in the bankers group knew others who were in the restaurant when Vivian left. Jesse thought it was a long shot but said he would do it. He was dialing Sam's number by the time Dave left the newsroom.

Chapter 33

Sam Slocum was one up on Jesse by the time Stallings called. He had already anticipated the questions to be asked and had found out there had been perhaps a hundred and fifty patrons at the restaurant while Vivian Blaine was there. There were seventeen people in the bankers' party, reducing the number of possible contacts to only a hundred and thirty-three. A party of fifteen garden club women whose names could be found reduced the number of unknowns to a hundred and eighteen. Jesse knew Janice would know some of them and could find the names of the others. He called and asked her to begin the process. She called back ten minutes later and said she had a list of all fifteen women.

Five minutes later, Devlin called back. He had just come from the restaurant and had met with the owner, Alex Karamanlis, and a few of the waiters. The manager,

Al for short, had given him a list of nearly fifty regular customers whose names could be checked via their credit card receipts. He was reluctant to do so at first because of the liability of invading the privacy of his customers. But when Devlin mentioned Vivian's name as the one he was trying to find, Karamanlis relented.

"I know her," he said. "Very beautiful lady. Very striking, could be Greek. Like Helena."

"That's the one," Devlin said.

"Oh, sure, I do anything to help find her. She's a very good customer, comes in once or twice a week a week for lunch, usually with some business man. All on the up and up, I'm sure. Sometimes I see her with the town attorney, what's his name, Wolf something. I think she works for him."

"That's the one," Devlin repeated.

"When did you say she was here last time?" Karmanlis asked.

"About a week ago. She was with a party of bankers and lawyers."

"Oh, of course. I remember seeing her that night. Dressed really nice, very sexy. She was talking to one of the garden club members."

"She wasn't with the bankers?"

"Oh sure, earlier in the evening. But later I saw her talking to a lady in the garden club group."

"Do you remember who it was?"

"I don't know their names."

"What did she look like?"

"I told you already. Very striking, like very fine Greek lady."

"No, not Vivian. What did the garden club woman look like?"

"I don't remember. Plain maybe. No, she was nice looking, too. Dark brown hair, short. Too short for my taste. Nice figure, though."

"How do you know what her figure was like?"

"I saw her leave her table right after speaking to Mrs. Blaine. Probably went to the restroom."

"What was she wearing?"

"A suit I think".

"A pant suit?"

"Yeah, that's it. A black pant suit."

"Anything else you noticed about her?"

"She seemed a little nervous. Maybe like she was upset."

"Jeez, Alex, your powers of observation are something. You sure you're not a private detective?

Karmanlis beamed. "Not really. I just remember fine looking women. It's a hobby. I'm a happily married man, but I can still look, can't I."

"Of course," said Devlin. "That's what makes the world go round." And round and round and round, he thought.

The P.I. left the steakhouse with the sense that he might have narrowed the search for the mystery woman down to one. Perhaps all he needed to do now was find out who that woman was. The list of two hundred suspects had been reduced to one member of the fifteen garden club women who had been at Out West that night. He left the restaurant, got in his car, apologized to Mary for taking so long. He then dialed Jesse's office number on his cell phone.

Jesse answered almost immediately.

"Jesse, this is Devlin. I think I've got it. If my hunch is right there's just a little more checking to do."

"What have you found, Dave?"

"I won't go into details now, but I think our mystery driver is a garden club member. Alex Karamanlis saw Vivian talking to her not long before she left the restaurant. He said the woman seemed agitated, perhaps as if something had upset her. You making any headway finding out who's in the garden club?"

"I don't know yet. Janice is working on it. She'll call me as soon as she knows anything."

"Okay, Jesse. I'm headed home now. Oh, wait a minute. What kind of car does Vivian drive?

"I think it's a two-door Chevy Malibu. Why?"

"Because it's the middle of the day and there's a two-door Chevy Malibu sitting here in the Out West parking lot. I'll get the license number and check with the PD to see if it might be Vivian's car."

"Good. Call me if any of our hunches turn out right."

Chapter 34

Back at Cee Edmunds' cabin near the lake, Vivian Blaine was slowly recuperating. The tissue around her eye was beginning to lose some of its reddish-blue tint and her breathing was a little easier. Cee had shaved most of the hair around the gash on her forehead and had pulled the skin into place, poured iodine on the wound and taped it together with masking tape, the only adhesive he had. Cee brought her a cup of hot green tea and a couple of buttered biscuits for breakfast. Seeing Cee with clear eyes for the first time since she had arrived at the cabin, Vivian was startled at first. "Who are you?" she asked.

"Cee," Edmunds replied.

"See what?"

"Just Cee," said Edmunds. "My name is Charles Edmunds, but most people just call me Cee."

"How long have I been here?"

"Nearly a week."

"Oh, my God. My family. They don't know where I am, do they? How did I get here?"

"I found you in the woods last week. You were unconscious."

"How long had I been there."

"I don't know. Maybe a day or two."

"Have you told anyone?"

"No."

"Why not?"

"I thought you needed to rest."

"Didn't you realize someone would miss me?"

"Yes."

"Then why didn't you contact someone?"

"Who?"

"I don't know—a doctor, the police, anyone."

"They might have thought I injured you."

"Why?"

"Most people think I'm strange."

"Are you?"

"Maybe."

"You didn't molest me, did you?"

"No."

"Are you normal?"

"What's normal?"

"Good question."

"Can I get you anything?"

"How about a telephone?"

"I don't have one."

"You don't have a phone?"

"Yes."

"Then you have one?"

"Yes, I don't have one."

"Jeez, Cee, you are strange."

"What do you do when you want to talk to someone?"

"I go and see them."

"Then you have a car?"

"No."

"You don't have a telephone and you don't have a car. What do you have?"

"Legs."

"You walk everywhere?"

"Yes."

"How am I lying here having this conversation with an idiot when people are wondering where I am?" Vivian said to herself. "I need to get up and get out of here. I need to call Ernie and let him know I'm all right. I need to talk to my children." Her head was beginning to hurt. Consciousness was slipping away again. "Please, God. Don't let this happen. Let me get out of here and let someone know that I'm not dead."

Vivian's eyes closed and she faded into sleep. Cee felt her forehead. It was warm but not hot. She was getting better. She would be all right, eventually.

Cee went back into the kitchen and filled a china cup with water from the sink and put it in a small microwave oven. He set the timer for a minute and a half, pressed the start button and reached into an overhead cabinet and got down a box of tea bags. Afterward, he went to the small refrigerator beside the cabinets, opened the door and took out a plastic bag containing several precooked biscuits and a container of margarine. He opened a drawer, got out a sharp knife, sliced the biscuits into top and bottom halves, spread each with margarine and put them buttered-side up in a counter-top toaster oven. He turned the oven on, went back to the refrigerator and removed a jar of seedless strawberry jam. A couple of seconds later the microwave timer dinged. Cee took out the cup of hot water, put the teabag in the water and placed it on the counter next to the toaster oven. When it looked as dark as a blood-red moon he removed the teabag, put two teaspoons of sugar in the hot liquid and sat down at the kitchen table to wait for the biscuits to warm. When they were done, he got up, took out the biscuits and spread each with a generous portion of strawberry jam. He sat back down at the table and ate the two biscuits and drank the hot tea very slowly. As soon as the biscuits were gone, he cleaned off the table, disposed of the paper towel he had used as a plate, picked up the tea and headed into a small alcove he used as a laundry room and office. Built into the wall on the opposite side of a washer and dryer was a counter top lined with books and offset by a two-year-old desktop computer.

Cee turned on the monitor, then the computer. He sipped his tea while he waited for the machine's programs to load. When they were ready, he opened a fractal generator program that displayed full-color creations of the Mandelbrot Set graphic patterns. He punched several numbers into the program parameter boxes and waited for the computer to begin creating seemingly random but fascinating images on the monitor screen. Once an image was complete, Cee used his mouse to move a rectangular box about an inch square to a portion of the image. He clicked on the left mouse button to magnify that portion of the image. What appeared on the screen was a fascinating enlargement of the image with tentacled offshoots that appeared as mutated extensions of the original. With each new click of the mouse, the image expanded and grew as if it were a biological entity. Enlarged portions of the expanded pieces resembled the roots and limbs of plants or trees, others looked like astronomical bodies. To Cee the amazing thing was that the extensions of the images were potentially infinite. Depending upon the speed and capacity of the computer processor, the images could be modified and expanded indefinitely. If one were able to print them on paper, the size of the paper would have to be bigger than the universe itself.

In the images Cee saw the same kind of infinite, multicolored patterns he had seen in the eddies and swirls of the water in the creek bed near the Conners Hill Elementary School as a young boy. It was from them that he had drawn his basic philosophy that the varieties of imperfection were the perfection of life itself. In his mind it was a recognition that the universe is a constant swirl of ever-changing creation with seemingly regular patterns but no apparent ultimate destination or stability—a chaotic world without end. He reasoned that if everything was totally constant and ordered, life ultimately would be dull and boring. It was the constant change that gave the world everything that appealed to the mind and the senses. It was always sensational and awesome, never dull and boring.

Cee realized there was a downside to his theory, however. The polar opposite of extreme perfection was extreme imperfection. The opposite of beauty was ugliness, the opposite of life, death; of creation, destruction. Death and destruction were built-in parts of life and creation. They could not be otherwise, for everything was a part of the whole, and every thing was a part of a "no-thing something," matter and anti-matter, existence and non-existence, materialness and emptiness.

The ultimate question in Cee's mind was not what existed or did not exist, but why. If God created the universe and all that was in it, why? What was the purpose? What purpose did life serve? Perhaps some of the theorists were right. Perhaps God created the world to serve Himself, to prove that He was God, to have individuals become like Him, to have a family of children that would look up to Him and worship Him as God. But why? Why did God need the love and adoration of children?

Cee Edmunds was a strange man. He had pondered such questions day and night from the time he was able to read and write. The answers, he believed, were as perplexing as the questions. As he grew into manhood, the questions became the answers. It had not occurred to him until he was almost fifty that "Why?" was not a question at all. It was an answer. To ask the question was to answer it, to give purpose to life. To give it purpose, one had to ask what purpose was to be served. And, of course, the answers were as varied as the questions. The purpose of life was to live, to grow, to learn, to suffer, to die. The purpose of life was to observe the process, to question it, to create it, to destroy it, to create it again, and again, and again. And ultimately to ask: Why?

Chapter 35

While Cee continued to nurse Vivian back to health, Jesse Stallings and others continued to look for the missing woman. The search had become a kind of community project that called into action the resources of various people. Among the most concerned were Sam Slocum, Vincent Sigman, Wolf Johnson and, of course, Ernie Blaine. Police Chief Stanfield Grady and Mayor Robert Ziglar were also concerned. A missing person in a small town could be blot on the town's image, and Ziglar, always the savvy politician, seemed more concerned with the town's image than his own. Stallings, invariably in search of a good story, and Devlin, the inveterate investigator, were becoming more involved on a professional level. Both wanted to solve the case to satisfy their curiosity and their intellectual egos.

But others were involved in the search as well, although unbeknown to the principal searchers. Despite his seeming disinterest in the case, Kingston Armour was making inquiries behind the scenes. He was talking to his partners and financiers in the real estate business, trying to find out what they might know about how and why Vivian had disappeared. He didn't expect to uncover much, but he knew Vivian had made friends with many of his peers in the business and that the mixture of business and pleasure of the type for which Vivian was known did not usually turn out well. In fact, the "King," as he was often called, was aware of several instances in which too much familiarity with a client's wife, husband or secretary had soured a money-making deal. Sexual philandering was a constantly available pitfall for any kind of businessman whose work took him away from the office and into the company of attractive clients on a regular basis.

Police officers often had similar problems. They were always on the move, constantly making contacts with people whose very nature was trouble. Jesse Stallings had seen more male police officers get into trouble with women than he cared to remember. One small town newspaper in North Carolina had once carried stories side by side on the front page about two seemingly separate subjects. The headline of one story read: Mayor's Wife Disappears. The headline on the other read: Town's Police Chief Resigns. Stallings had even heard rumors that members of the Conners Hill Police Department had engaged in sexual orgies as a group on occasion. He believed the story was most likely the fabrication of someone with a grievance against the department, but it had been repeated by so many people, including one policeman himself, that it was difficult to dismiss.

As a reader of many short stories and novels, Jesse knew that the main ingredients of most first-degree murders usually came down to just three things: lust, greed and power. Of the three, sexual lust was the easiest to understand. Power and greed were something else. They derived more often than not from the subtlest psychological conditions. What made a man or woman throw everything to the wind in a grab for money or power? Jesse had some ideas and opinions based on a lifetime of reading and observing human nature, but none of them fit every possible situation. More important perhaps, the situations, like the elements of the universe, were as diverse and far-flung as one could imagine. In actuality, they were probably more subtle, more numerous and more widespread than one could imagine. They were as great or greater than the grains of sand on all the beaches of all the oceans of the world.

Stallings was beginning to sense that deep inside Vivian Blaine's attempt to become a power player in the community was some hidden psychological agenda. She was too intelligent a woman to throw caution to the wind for some temporary sexual gratification. That kind of commodity was more often a man's undoing than a woman's, although the reverse could be true. There were no hard and fast rules regulating human physical behavior. Every case could be different, and usually was. What was Vivian after and how did she intend to get it? Jesse wondered.

Somehow Ernie's Blaine's wife had caused a major ripple in the fabric of the Conners Hill community. Never had the town's newspaper editor heard so much speculation and gossip among the male population. It was as if the rumor mill, once subtle and subdued, had erupted into a cacophonous buzz. Something besides the comings and goings of a seemingly wayward wife was no doubt behind it. But what? As always, Jesse wanted to know the whys and wherefores, even if he wasn't able to use the information in his work. It was a part of his being, almost an obsession. It would drive him crazy if he could not learn the story behind the story.

The trouble was: he had little to go on. He had no personal contact with Vivian and would have hardly known she existed had it not been that the Blaines were nearby neighbors. She had seldom come to church, and Jesse's work writing and editing newspaper copy kept him tied to his desk most of the time. As a reporter, he might have run into her every now and then. But now he learned of community events mostly through telephone calls and the stories reporters brought back to the paper. Even Janice was perplexed by the rumors. She had seen Vivian sporadically and had heard of some of her exploits. She often saw her walking with her children in the neighborhood but had not bothered to go and introduce herself. She wasn't sure why. Perhaps her own fragile self-image could not tolerate the thought of being compared to a woman so strikingly beautiful.

Do we, even as adults, never get over our childhood fears and jealousies? Jesse wondered.

Chapter 36

Just as Sam Slocum was beginning to feel that his efforts to create casino gambling in the state were succeeding, he was struck by the resistance of a few of Conners Hill's most powerful individuals. Interestingly, the reticence he encountered was not always that of ministers and their congregations, nor of those who felt that gambling was a bad thing per se. Much of it came from politicians and civic leaders who felt that gambling, while universal and inevitable, was a threat to the public welfare. They reasoned that the laws of economics were relatively simple and that if too much money left the pockets of average men and women and turned up in the coffers of corporate casinos, it would deprive other individuals and businesses of its use.

It was an argument that Owen Jobs, publisher of the Conners Hill News, often cited when referring to giant superstores or "big-box stores," as they were sometimes called. He thought the giant retail outlets were in the process of destroying small mom-and-pop stores of the nation by becoming economic sponges.

"Just look at what's happening," Jobs said to Jesse during one of their afternoon sessions. "A giant corporation opens up a superstore that offers customers everything, including things that have traditionally been handled by the small stores—things like clothes, jewelry, groceries, eye glasses, and the like. With their ability to buy in gigantic lots and thereby to sell at greatly reduced prices, they can undercut the prices of just about any small retail business there is. Hell, a big-box store can sell office supplies cheaper than we can buy them."

As usual, Jobs saw the threat not only to the mom-and-pop stores, but to his office supply business as well. Not only that, but he felt the big-box stores were a very real threat to his existence as a newspaper publisher. It was an indirect threat, to be sure, but it was extremely acute in one very real sense. All newspapers, whatever their size or circulation, existed primarily on the strength of their advertising sales. Newspapers brought in comparatively little revenue from individual or subscription sales of the papers themselves. The bulk of their revenue, perhaps eighty to ninety percent of it, came from advertisers. In small communities like Conners Hill, a good percentage of those advertisers were small retail businesses. If those businesses went out of business because of competition from the big-box stores, it was a direct loss for the newspaper. The fewer small retail stores, the fewer number of small town advertisers.

The general public often did not understand the relationship between publishing and advertising. A bright young engineer from one of the town's large manufacturers once remarked to Jesse that he liked very much the free tabloid shopper that had just been published. Stallings responded that the owners were doing a very good job but that the shopper could be a threat to the News' existence.

"Why is that?" the engineer inquired. "The only thing they print is advertising. You are in the news business."

Jesse had to explain that if the newspaper lost too much of its advertising revenue, it could no longer exist as a newspaper. "The amount of money we make from the sale of newspapers themselves covers hardly more than the cost of paper and ink. It's advertising that pays for the salaries of reporters and editors, for production workers, for newspaper deliveries, computers and printing presses."

In his early days with the Conners Hill News, even Jesse did not understand the economics of newspaper publishing. When the Selwin Daily Mirror, the county's only daily newspaper, began publishing a small paper in Conners Hill, Owen Jobs was livid. "They are out to destroy us," he said to Jesse.

Jesse ignorantly argued that the Mirror's owners had no such intention. He had read the Selwin paper as long as he could remember. His picture had even appeared in the paper on occasion during high school, usually with some sports story concerning the Conners Hill High School football team. "After all, they've been the only daily newspaper in the county for more than eighty years. They've always printed a good bit of the news in Conners Hill," he said to Jobs.

"Of course, they aren't really out to destroy our business," Jobs replied. "They just want to take away as much of our advertising as possible, which would destroy our business."

Jesse had to acknowledge that Jobs was right. Destroy their advertising revenue and newspapers would go the way of the dinosaur. He was beginning to see the truth of it more and more as the Internet began to take the advertising dollars of more and more newspapers.

There were other leaders who saw the dangers of corporate casinos as well. As a developer and church leader, Greg Irwin knew all too well the drain on public resources that a major gambling operation could be. People who spent money in casinos had less money to spend on other things, including house payments, rent, business investments and the like. Some of them had less money to spend on the necessities of life themselves, things such as food, clothes, water and sewer services, telephone bills, etc. They also gave less to the church and to charitable organizations in general.

Irwin, who had been very successful as a businessman, was a master of practical economics. He understood that money itself is a commodity. Most people were limited by the sources of their income and their ability to adjust their lifestyles to balance income and expenses. His motto was simple: Earn more or spend less. "Spend less than you earn and you will one day be financially independent," he advised young protégés. "And remember, you can't buy happiness with money or things. Happiness is not a commodity; it is a frame of mind."

The problem for Slocum was that in Conners Hill, people like Irwin and Mayor Ziglar carried a lot of political weight. Ziglar, in particular, could stifle a major movement with little more than a nod of his head. Part of his influence was due to the fact that he had grown up in the town, had paid his dues both in terms of political and public service and was generally regarded as perhaps the most intrinsically intelligent man ever to hold the mayor's office. Moreover, he was a people's politician. Though one of the brightest students ever to attend Conners Hill High School, he had chosen not to attend college. After a brief stint in the Navy, he had come back to Conners Hill and had thrown himself into the political arena with a verve that few could match. With an almost photographic memory and the ability to sort out complex problems and lay out solutions in the simplest terms, he had, in 25 years as the town's mayor, become an almost invincible leader.

Slocum was finding the mayor a somewhat perplexing adversary. On the surface, Ziglar appeared to be for most any new idea that would enhance the growth and reputation of the community, perhaps even for the gambling community if it would produce a better town. But underneath, Ziglar had major reservations. He had seen individual gamblers come and go. Usually they left with less than they had come with. Gamblers, he felt, were dreamers at heart. They dreamed of having great wealth at little expense. They dreamed of becoming rich and powerful without any real notion as to what they would do with wealth and power.

Ziglar, on the other hand, was a practical man. He understood that wealth and power were mere accouterments of successful people—that success, like happiness, was a relative term. A happy man, he believed, was a wealthy man, not because he had money and expensive things but because he was content with himself. A happy man was one who was content no matter what his station in life. As a result, the mayor surrounded himself with little of what many considered the finer things in life. He operated an insurance business out of a small office in a mobile trailer. It contained a sofa and two chairs for clients and a desk and chair for himself. The desk was orderly but partially covered with stacks of papers. He had no computer, nor did he want one. His primary database was his brain, which was filled with thousands, perhaps millions, of bits of information which he could bring up at a second's notice. He had never learned to type and relied on a trusted secretary to put most of his thoughts on paper. He could usually access the thoughts from memory.

Slocum's problem was that Ziglar did not fully trust him. The mayor had an uncanny knack for reading the character of a man simply by listening to him. Some little something, perhaps a slip of the tongue here or a misspoken reference there, was all Ziglar needed. On a personal level, the mayor found Slocum intelligent, witty and charming, but he believed Slocum's wit and charm masked a darker side. It was the same dark side he found in many of the people who were driven toward wealth and power. In Ziglar's mind, it was an attempt to compensate for something that was missing. In many it manifested itself in a relatively harmless ambition. In a few it bordered on the edge of psychosis. In them, it dominated their every thought and produced an inflexible determination to have their own way.

Robert Ziglar believed Sam Slocum was an individual who had vowed to let nothing stand in his way and to do whatever was necessary to clear the path toward eventual success. He was, in Ziglar's mind, capable of nothing less than murder if he thought it necessary to accomplish his goal. Such thoughts Ziglar found troubling if not repulsive, for the mayor, though a man of ambition and determination himself, was a pragmatic realist who never let his own thinking override his perception of ultimate reality. To the mayor, the acceptance of ultimate reality was an acceptance of the world as it was, not as he wished it to be. The ultimate realist, he believed, was a person willing to put ideas and concepts—and perhaps even his principles—aside if they conflicted with the public interest. Like Franklin Roosevelt, Ziglar could "walk with the devil" if circumstances required it, for to him the devil appeared in many disguises, one of them being, on occasion, an angelic advocate of things noble and good.

Ziglar would continue to listen to the arguments of Slocum regarding casino gambling and to keep an open mind as to their merits. But an open mind, like an open door, needed a screen when the weather demanded it. Without a screen, unhealthy thoughts flew into a person's mind the same way flies of summer flew into an open door.

Chapter 37

After his breakfast with Jesse at Charlie's, Cee felt a wave of remorse. Listening to Stallings' tell of the psychological effects he had suffered from not getting a college paper in on time, Edmunds realized that the smallest aberration in one's pattern of behavior, or even in one's pattern of thinking, could have serious long-term effects. He knew now that he had to let someone know where Vivian was and that she was all right, both for her sake and for her family's. He left Charlie's and began the two-mile trek back to his cottage near the lake. On the way he reflected on his thinking and particularly on the fact that his feelings were approaching the level of guilt for not having let someone know about Vivian sooner. Guilt was not something Cee often entertained. Somewhere he had once read that guilt was "the price one pays for doing something one shouldn't have done so that he can do it again." Once you have paid the price of guilt for having committed some sin, you are free to sin again. As much as Cee abhorred the notion that sin was anything more than a psychological aberration itself, he could not escape his moral upbringing in a proper Southern family. Sometimes he felt guilty merely for feeling guilty. But he could not control his feelings any more than he could control his thinking about them. His thoughts were racing as he headed north on Main Street toward the railroad tracks. His legs were trying to catch up.

In the meantime, Jesse returned to the newspaper office. He called Janice to ask if she had any more news about the women in the garden club. Before he could reach her, however, he received a call from Dave Devlin. When he answered the phone, Dave sounded excited.

"Jesse, I think we may have our woman," the P.I. gushed. "I just got a call from one of the waiters at Out West. He knows who Vivian may have left the restaurant with the night the bankers met. I'm going to do a little more checking. I'll drop by and give you the details. You might want to get in touch with Janice and see if she's found out anything more."

"Dave, can't you give me a little something to go on before you get here. If I reach Janice, I'll need a name so she can give me some background about her."

"Sure, but it's not much so far. The only name the waiter could remember was a Mrs. Seemore. He didn't know her first name, but he believes she owns some kind of shop downtown."

"Nan Seemore? Was that it? She owns a gift shop in Cletus Lampley's little mini-mall just off Main Street near Wolf Johnson's office."

"I don't know if that's the one or not, but it sounds like it may be. What does she look like?"

"She's an attractive woman in her late thirties or early forties. She has dark brown hair, almost black in fact. She wears it short and combed back like a duck-tail some guys back in the fifties used to wear. I think at one time she was president of the garden club. In fact, she may still be president. We took a photo of the club's officers not too long ago and, as far as I can remember, she was in the picture. I'll see if I can dig it up."

"That's great, Jesse. In the meantime, see if Janice can come up with anything that might give us a clue as to why she and Vivian were talking."

"I'll let you know just as soon as I've talked to Janice."

"Good. I think we may be on to something. Oh, by the way, Jesse, where does this Seemore woman live? We'll need to know that if our hunches turn out to be right."

"I think she and her husband Jonah have a house out near the Conners Hill Lake. There are a couple of roads that wind through the woods around the lake. It's very quiet and peaceful out there. I wanted to buy a house there myself once, but it was a little too expensive for my blood. And that was before real estate prices around here started to hit the roof."

"Sounds interesting, Jesse. What does Seemore's husband do, by the way?"

"He's a banker."

CHAPTER 38

It was nearly noon when Cee reached home. He found Vivian sitting at the kitchen table sipping on a cup of hot green tea, munching on a cold biscuit and mumbling incoherently to herself. She had on the T-shirt and the pajama bottoms he had put her in shortly after bringing her to the cabin.

"What the hell have I been up to?" she said offhandedly as Cee entered the room. Her words seemed directed as much to herself as to Cee, however. She was looking at him, but her gaze seemed focused somewhere else. "What could I have been thinking?"

"Perhaps you've been thinking too much," said Cee. "Thinking is the bane of the civilized world. It's our thinking that causes all the trouble—that and language."

Vivian stared at him as if he were a fool.

"What I mean by that is that we come into the world with no language at all. We are fresh and untainted, totally innocent. And then we begin to learn to walk and talk. The walking is good, the talking not so good."

Vivian continued to stare at him as if he were crazy.

"What do you mean that talking is not so good," she said. "If we couldn't talk, we couldn't communicate. We wouldn't be able to read or write or learn anything about each other. We'd be like the earliest cavemen, all puffed up and no place to go, no coherent thought, no ideas, no vision of what it is we want to have or to accomplish. Where would that have gotten us?"

"Where has all the talk gotten us?" Cee responded. "Are we better off now than Adam and Eve were in the Garden of Eden? I'm not so sure."

"Adam and Eve were dummies," said Vivian. "What did they know? They had paradise all to themselves and they botched it. They screwed it up for the rest of us."

"How did they do that?" asked Cee.

"Well, obviously it wasn't by talking. They screwed it up by committing the ultimate sin, the one we keep doing over and over."

"What is that?"

"Well, if you don't know, I'm certainly not going to tell you."

"No, I'm serious," said Cee. "What was their original sin? Was it running around naked all the time? Was it fornicating whenever and wherever they wanted? Or was it something more basic?"

"What do you mean?"

"Was it what they did or what they thought about what they did?"

"What was there to think about? They just did it and that was that."

"Are you sure?"

"Of course, I'm sure. What else could it have been?"

"Well, think about it."

"I thought you didn't like thinking."

"I don't dislike thinking. It's a natural thing to do."

"So what don't you like?"

"I don't like thinking that our thinking is reality. I don't like thinking that words are reality. They're just the symbols of reality, not reality itself."

"Now, you're really beginning to sound like an idiot."

"Well, think about it. When I use the word 'table' I am thinking of a table, right?"

"Of course, what else could a table be?"

"But what table is it that I'm thinking about? Is it this breakfast table, or a coffee table, a dining room table or an end table? Or maybe it's a table of contents or a writing table."

Vivian threw up her hands and looked toward the ceiling as if to say 'Oh, God, why me?" Instead she gave Cee another chance to explain himself.

"Okay, Cee. What exactly has this got to do with original sin? How did we get from sin to thinking.? I'm a little confused."

"Well, again, think about it. What was the sin?"

"Eve ate the forbidden fruit and she talked Adam into eating some of it, and life hasn't been the same since."

"And what was that fruit?"

Perfect Imperfection

"I think it was an apple. What do you think?"

"I think the apple was a symbol of something else."

"You mean like sex?"

"Not necessarily."

"Then what?"

"The Bible makes it pretty clear, but most of us have forgotten what it says."

"What does it say?"

"It says Eve ate the 'fruit of the tree of knowledge'."

"Are you saying that knowledge is the source of all our problems?

"Pretty much."

"But where would we be without knowledge."

"Most likely, we'd still be in paradise. A very simple, imperfect paradise, but still paradise. No doubt we'd still be animals, like all the other animals, which pretty much still live in paradise."

"Oh, Jesus, Cee. How can an animal live in paradise when they don't even know what paradise is?"

"And we do?"

"Well, of course. It's a place that's perfect. A place that's beautiful, ideal, where there's no crime or hate, where it's comfortable and cozy all the time and nobody gets sick or dies."

"Do animals hate other animals and commit crimes? Do they understand what an ideal is? Do they know what is happening when they are sick or about to die? Do they worry about dying? Do they think about an ideal place and wish they could go there?"

"Probably not."

"Why not?"

"They have no knowledge of such things."

"Exactly."

"But Cee, we are not animals. We are human beings who think."

"There, you have it!"

"What?"

"The source of all our problems."

Chapter 39

At the Conners Hill News Jesse was trying to find out all he could about Nan Seemore and her husband, Jonah. Janice had filled him in as to some of the details of the family history. What she knew was sketchy, but it was more than Jesse had known before. The Seemores had lived in the town for more than fifteen years and were well respected by most of the community. Jonah was the manager of a local branch bank and active in the affairs of the Chamber of Commerce and several civic organizations. Raised in the Deep South, he tended to be politically conservative and had no doubt been a Democrat before the civil rights movement and the integration of the public schools. Once the conservative movement gained ground in the South, he tactfully called himself a "registered Democrat" and finally a Republican. Nan, also a Southerner and, if anything, somewhat more conservative than her husband, had been an outspoken critic of integration. Once it was put in place by federal mandate she had insisted that their only daughter attend a private church-run school on the outskirts of town.

Nan was the more socially active member of the family. She kept herself busy not only in the local garden club but in the Friends of the Library, the Woman's Club, a church circle and several book clubs. She was more than happy to express her opinion about almost anything and everything and did so frequently, whether her opinion was asked for or not. In recent years, her most vitriolic criticism had been toward the increasingly open attitude of the so-called "gay" community, which she often spoke of as "that abominable aberration." Most homosexuals she referred to simply as "queers." There were a number of women among her friends who held similar opinions but were either less outspoken or more tactful. A few regarded Nan as a thoughtless gossip. A few of their husbands refused to bank with Jonah simply because they knew the pain his wife's verbal outbursts had caused other members of the community. While they, too, believed homosexuality was an aberration and a sin, they recognized that it was also a fact of life and that whether one approved or disapproved, it was a sin that, like gluttony or adultery, could not be denied.

Jesse did not approve of homosexual activity and found even the thought of it repulsive, but he believed many of the facts of life, while disturbing, were part of the fabric of existence that could not be denied. Lust, envy, greed, hate, jealousy, righteousness—all were profane and disturbing elements of the human condition, but nonetheless real. If God disapproved of such things, would He have admitted them into the world to create social and political unrest and upheaval? The question, no doubt, was moot in that they were a part of the real world and apparently served some purpose.

"What more can you tell me about Nan Seemore?" Jesse asked when he had finally reached Janice on the phone.

"She's a two-faced bitch," Jan replied nonchalantly.

Jesse was startled. His wife was seldom so straightforward and almost never critical of others' behavior no matter how repugnant she found it.

"Jeez, Jan, what makes you say that? I thought you liked the woman? You once told me she was a real go-getter, one of the up and coming leaders of the community."

"I changed my mind," said Jan.

"Why?"

"Because she's a bitch."

"Would you please explain yourself. I can't believe you have such strong feelings about anyone."

"Well, I do about her."

"Why?"

"Because she thinks you are a spineless moron."

"What? What makes you think that?"

"She said so."

"She said that to you?"

"Not to me, no, but she said it."

"How do you know?"

"Bebe Bullis told me."

"How did Bebe know?"

"She was with her when she said it."

"Jan, maybe you're mistaken. Maybe that's not what Bebe said she heard. How do you know for sure?"

"Bebe told me she was out with Nan and a couple of other women and they were talking about one of your editorials—you know, the one about the war in Iraq and how it had given the country a black eye throughout the world—and she said the editorial was an example of a moronic attack on President Bush's foreign policy strategy."

"Then she didn't actually say I was a moron, she just said the editorial was moronic?"

"No, she said you were a moron for having written it."

"Bebe said that?"

"No, Bebe said Nan said it."

"And you believe it?"

"Believe what?"

"That Nan actually said that."

"Of course, she says stuff like that all the time."

"She's never said anything like that to me."

"Of course not. That's why she's a two-faced bitch. She says one thing to your face and another to your back."

"Well, some of my editorials do make me sound like a moron sometimes."

"Of course, but that's not the point."

"What is the point?"

"That Nan Seemore is a bitch."

Jesse realized he wasn't going to get much further in his quest for information about Nan Seemore. His wife Janice was often emotional and illogical but seldom wrong. He would bet that her opinion of Seemore involved more than the seemingly trivial report of Nan's criticism of an editorial. He didn't have time at the moment to pursue the possibility that she was leaving something out of the mix. He had no idea of what it was, but whatever the case, Janice was not one of Seemore's admirers. He decided to end the conversation, but before doing so, he remembered Devlin's request and asked one further question.

"Janice, do you happen to know where Nan and Jonah Seemore live?"

"Of course, Jesse, and so should you."

"Why is that?"

"Because we went to a party at their house one Christmas eve. You know, they live in a lovely A-frame house off Barrister Drive near Conners Hill Lake Park."

"Oh, yeah, now I remember. It's up on a hill about a quarter of a mile above the lake."

"Yeah, that's the one."

"I remember going there. I just couldn't remember whose house it was."

"Jesse, dear, you are a moron!."

Jesse wondered why the road near the lake was called Barrister Drive. No doubt some lawyer had either owned the land or had built the first house on it and he couldn't think of anything better to name it.

Chapter 40

Stallings wondered what possible connection there might be between Nan Seemore and Vivian Blaine. Moreover he wondered why Nan might have become upset at something Vivian said to her the night of the bankers' dinner at Out West. He realized it might have had nothing to do with Vivian's disappearance or with whatever had been going on in either of their lives, but the fact that something had happened between them, however trivial or insignificant, was the only clue he and Dave Devlin had at the moment. As far as they knew, Vivian's brief conversation with Nan had come only a short time before Vivian left the restaurant. It was the last time anyone had seen Nan in the past week. If she had left the garden club group early to meet Vivian in the parking lot, some other club member attending their outing would probably know it. If Nan hadn't left the group, Jesse and Dave had reached another dead end.

Jesse picked up the phone and dialed Dave's number. Devlin, as usual, answered the phone after the first ring.

"Devlin Investigative Services, Dave speaking."

"Hey, Dave, Jesse here. Jeez, man, you must live by the telephone."

"Only when I'm working, pretty much all the time."

"Sorry to bother you again," said Jesse. I'm just checking to see if you've picked up anything new about Vivian. I may have a little something for you, but I'm not sure. Janice gave me some background information on Nan Seemore, but nothing substantial. Oh, she did tell me that the Seemores live on Barrister Road above the town lake off Old Valley School Road. You know the place?'

"Not their house, but I'm familiar with the road. Did some work once for an attorney who lives out there. Nice, quiet neighborhood."

"Yeah, that's the one. Anyway, according to Janice, that's where Seemore and her husband live. You found out anything more about Nan?"

"Yeah, a little. I know her husband Jonah is a banker and that he and his wife moved to Conners Hill about fifteen years ago. I did a little Internet checking and found that they came here from Atlanta, Georgia. I called an attorney friend down there with some longtime connections in the area and he was very helpful. In fact, he knew some people who knew the Seemores—well, not exactly the Seemores—but Nan Seemore's family, the Newbeaus."

"Newbeau, doesn't exactly sound like an old Southern name."

"It isn't, and it wasn't before it was changed from Nussbaum to Newbeau."

"Nussbaum? That sounds German."

"It is. It's a German Jewish name but one that spells good old Southern money."

"How's that?"

"Because Gottfried Nussbaum, the father of Isaac Nussbaum, Nan's great-grandfather, the patriarch of the family, moved to Georgia from New York in the early 1800s to live in a warmer climate and seek his fortune in the cotton business. He was a very smart old cookie, and it wasn't long before he had turned a couple of small farms into a conglomerate of highly profitable plantations and a string of warehouses and mercantile stores that sold cotton dry goods. He died not long after Sherman marched through Atlanta, but his family held onto the plantations and retail stores and they have maintained the businesses and their social prominence ever since. Nan's father had his name changed to Newbeau when he was a young man. Nan was raised as a Newbeau."

"Why was that?"

"Well, despite their wealth and their political prominence, the Nussbaums were never totally accepted by the Old South society in Atlanta. The mere fact that Gottfried Nussbaum had moved there from New York and was Jewish made them suspect. Nan Newbeau grew up feeling wealthy but deprived. Though in 1850 Jews made up only one percent of Atlanta's population of just over 2,500 people, they owned more than 10 percent of the retail businesses in the city. Jewish businessmen found an easy acceptance into the life of the community until the early 1900s, when Leo Frank was convicted of murdering a female worker in his pencil factory. He was lynched by a mob but later pardoned. That, plus the fact that many Jewish store owners often sold goods to blacks and sometimes hired them to work in their stores did not go over well with a society still rooted in the prejudices of its slave-holding past."

"So, Dave, what does all this have to do with the Seemores?" Jesse asked.

"Not too much, except that in order to remove her from some of the more unseemly aspects of Southern prejudice, Nan's family sent her away to a private school. Apparently, instead of learning to mingle with the general public and to develop a compassionate egalitarian attitude toward ordinary people, she followed the path of her more natural inclinations. which were decidedly self-defensive and egocentric. I think she ended the battle between her ingrained self-doubt and her normally outgoing nature by becoming an outspoken but highly conservative gossip-monger."

"I still don't see what this has to do with the disappearance of Vivian Blaine," said Jesse.

"I don't either," Dave admitted, "except that we know that Nan might have been the last person Vivian spoke to before she disappeared. Perhaps, Vivian got wind of something Nan had said about her and confronted her about it in front of her garden club friends at Out West and that touched off a private meeting between them."

Jesse paused to reflect. "I guess that could have happened, but why do you think Vivian told Vincent

Sigman she was planning to pick up some beer for Ernie when she left the restaurant?"

"I have no idea, Jesse," Devlin replied. "Perhaps something said at the garden club table that night could give us a clue. Why don't you ask Janice to do a little prying into that one? Maybe something was said that struck a chord with someone."

"Sounds reasonable," said Jesse. "I'll talk to Janice and have her do a little checking."

Chapter 41

Before picking up the phone to call Janice, Stallings began looking through the mail on his desk. In the middle of the stack was a plain white envelope with his name on it. It had no stamp and no return address, and he immediately wondered where it came from. He ran his letter opener under the flap of the envelope and pulled out a single sheet of paper. There were just three words scrawled on it:

She's with me.

"What the hell?" Jesse mumbled to himself. "Who's with whom?"

He could think of only one person who might write such a cryptic message, but before drawing any conclusions, he punched the button for the News' business office intercom. Becky Martin answered right away..

"Becky, this is Jesse. I've got a piece of mail here that I don't understand. It has no stamp and no return address. It was apparently hand-delivered. Do you have any idea where it came from?"

"Sure, Jesse, it's from that fellow, Cee something. He brought it by early this morning. He asked for you, but I told him you hadn't come in yet. He acted a little nervous about giving it to me, but I told him I'd put it in your stack of mail and you'd probably see it as soon as you got here. I think that was enough to satisfy him."

"Thanks, Becky. At least now I know it probably isn't from some nut case."

"You don't think Cee whatever-his-name-is is a nut case? Seems to me if he's not a little off his rocker, he may be missing a few digits in his genetic code."

"Becky, that's not like you. You don't seem to mind the rest of us genetically-impaired nut cases. What's so different about Cee?"

"Well, for one thing, he seldom says anything, and if he does, it's usually not anything I can understand. When he came in this morning, I asked him how he was doing and he didn't answer me. He just handed me the envelope. Then he stood there looking at me as if I was supposed to say something. When I asked if there was something else he needed, he just nodded and pointed toward the letter and then toward the door. When I said I didn't understand, he pointed toward the clock in the office. Finally, I realized what he wanted and I asked him just to make sure."

"What did he want?"

"He wanted to know what time you would be here."

"What did you tell him?"

"I said you might have worked late last night and that you'd probably be in around ten o'clock. He just nodded and left. He never said a word while he was here."

"Well, Becky, that's just Cee's way. He's not fond of words. He thinks they're an impediment to understanding."

"How's that?"

"He says words are just symbols of reality, not reality itself. You know, kind of like the guy who said 'the map is not the territory'."

"Who was that?"

"The philosopher Alfred Korzybski."

"What did he mean by 'the map is not the territory?'"

"Well, you know, you can look at a map and see the outline of an area that's called North Carolina. But the map isn't North Carolina, it's just a line drawn around a scaled representation of an area we call North Carolina. If you fly over the state in an airplane, you don't see North Carolina, you just see the land with trees and fields and houses and so on. The map is just a concept we use to make laws, collect taxes, build roads—things like that."

"Okay, that makes sense—I think."

"Cee thinks we don't see what's real most of the time, or least we don't think about what's real. We just think about the concepts we have about what's real. Does that make sense?"

"Probably not, but I'm not one of those genetically-impaired nut cases like you and Cee."

"Thanks Becky. I love you, too."

Turning off the intercom Jesse wondered who was with Cee. As far as he knew, he had no lady friends and probably rarely, if ever, entertained visitors. Nonetheless, he wasn't a total recluse. He had done carpentry work for hundreds of people around town. Many of his customers found him strange but not difficult. He seldom charged more than a job was worth, and if someone was unhappy with the work, he redid it without whining or arguing about it. If they refused to pay him a reasonable amount, he didn't protest; he just made a mental note never to work for them again.

It hadn't occurred to Jesse that Cee's note might have been referring to Vivian. He recalled that he had mentioned her to Cee at least once, but he doubted whether Cee had ever met her. He was sure that if Cee had ever heard the stories about Vivian he would simply have listened, said nothing and forgotten what was said. As far as Edmunds was concerned, gossip was one of the thorns of small town life. Though it often amounted to nothing, it sometimes was the cause of wounded feelings and serious conflict. Cee himself was fond of talking about "nothing," but the nothing he talked about was that which he insisted was the basis of everything.

One of the few prolonged conversations Jesse ever had with Edmunds was about "nothingness," which Cee insisted was not nothingness per se but was better understood as "no-thing-ness." Cee tried to explain to Jesse that "no-thing-ness" was the sine qua non of everything, or in his words, that "in order for anything to exist, there must be an emptiness in which it can exist." Emptiness, or no-thing-ness, was, in his mind, the soul of spirituality: the surreal, inexplicable truth behind everything imaginable

Perfect Imperfection

and unimaginable. Of course, talking about such things was as pointless as searching for the end of a circle.

In fact, Cee was fascinated by circles, for as a youth he had found them to be graphical symbols of perfection. Like eternity, they were visible representations of something with no beginning and no end. Later, as a young man, he had run across a chart of photographs used by a plastic surgeon to explain the symmetrical basis of beautiful faces. The chart was comprised of eight photographs arranged in two rows of four. At the top left was the face of someone with facial disfigurements so irregular and unsymmetrical it appeared to be that of a grotesque monster. Each face after that was one in which the irregularities became less and less prominent until the eighth face, which was that of a beautiful British movie actress.

When Cee first looked at the chart he was stunned. It occurred to him that if the surgeon had added a third row to the chart and followed it to its logical conclusion, not only would the symmetry of the beautiful face have disappeared, but so would every other feature that it bore. The chin, nose, eyes and ears would all have become less and less pronounced, eventually to the point of extinction. The face at the end of the third row would have existed as nothing but a circle. It would have been, in Cee's mind, the picture of a perfect face.

Jesse argued with Cee that such a hypothesis was ridiculous.

"Let's take the logic of the semanticist who says the map is not the territory," he said. "If the map is not the territory, then the picture is not a person, correct?"

"Correct," Cee replied.

"Then if the picture is not the person, the circle is not the face of a person but is the mere conceptual representation of a face."

"Right."

"Then how can the circle be the face of a person?"

"It can't."

"Then where does that leave your argument?"

"At the point where most arguments begin."

"And where is that?"

"Where it is asserted that anything is absolutely and unequivocally what one says it is."

"Are you saying that if I assert that a face is a face, it is a face?"

"Of course."

"What if I say your ass is your face?"

"Then it is."

"Come on now, Cee. You know that's ridiculous."

"How so?"

"Because everyone knows that your ass is not your face."

"Oh, but they don't."

"You mean some people think you look like an ass?"

"Absolutely."

"Okay, I'll accept that. But what about the proposition that anybody's ass is their face? It's obviously untrue."

"I'll accept that if you will agree that what something is, is what everybody agrees that it is."

"You are saying that if everybody agrees that a face is an ass, then it is an ass."

"Yes."

Perfect Imperfection

"Aren't we just getting back to semantics? Aren't we just explaining words with other words we like better."

"Absolutely."

"So where does that leave us?"

"Back at the beginning of a circle."

"Which is?"

"Nowhere."

Chapter 42

As soon as Jesse returned to his cubicle on the second floor of the News building, he picked up the phone to call Cee. Before he could do so, however, Becky paged him.

"Jesse, Janice is on line one."

"Thanks, Becky."

He punched the lighted button on the telephone..
"Hey, Hon, what's up?"

"Just thought you'd like to know I've got some information for you about Nan."

"Good, I was just about to call you and let you know Dave Devlin has come up with some stuff as well. He's almost certain we're on the right track. We just need to know a little bit more about whether Nan and Vivian talked at Out West the night she disappeared. Of course it wouldn't hurt to know what they talked about either."

"Well, that's what I was calling you about. It seems they did speak to one another briefly."

"How do you know."

"Bebe was there. She said Vivian stopped by their table. She said Nan and Vivian exchanged some rather harsh words."

"Did she say what they were?"

"She said it all happened so quickly, she didn't understand what the conversation was about but that it apparently involved something between Vivian and one of Nan's friends."

"Did she know who the friend was?"

"Not really, but she said the exchange wasn't too pleasant. She said Nan told Vivian to lay off the friend's husband or she would find herself in big trouble. Actually, Bebe said Nan said something else, but I'm not going to repeat it."

"Why not?"

"It's not very nice."

"Hey, Jan. This is me, your husband. If you can't tell me, who can you tell?"

"Nobody."

"Did she give any indication who the husband was?"

"Not really, but she thought it might be someone who does business with Jonah's bank. Oh, wait a minute. She did mention a name. I think it was Larry."

"Jeez, there must be a dozen guys named Larry who do business with Jonah. That doesn't help a lot. Did Nan say anything else about Larry?"

"Only what I told you I couldn't tell you."

"Jan, this is important. What was it Nan said to Vivian?"

"Well, I'm not sure I heard Bebe right, but she said Nan said, 'If you don't keep your hands out of Larry's pants, you're gonna be sorry.'"

"Did Vivian say anything back to her."

"Yeah."

"Well, what was it?"

"Screw you, bitch."

"That's it."

"I'm sorry, Jesse, but that's all I've got, except that Bebe said Nan got so upset about the exchange that she excused herself and went to the ladies room. She said Nan must have been really upset because she never came back to the table. Apparently she left the restaurant."

"Did Bebe know what time it was when she left?"

"I didn't ask her, but I'll call her back and find out."

"Good work, Jan. Let me know as soon as you can."

"Okay, I'll get right on it."

"Oh, Jan, one other question."

"What's that?"

"Does Nan Seemore like beer?"

"Jesse, how would I know that?"

"I thought maybe you might have been out with the girls when there was some beer-drinking going on."

"I don't recall, but I doubt it. Most women I know aren't that crazy about beer. Why do you ask?"

"Just a hunch. Pat Tomlinson told me he dated a girl named Miller once who was from a German family and that she liked beer."

"Well, your hunch sounds like a long shot to me, but if Nan has some German roots, maybe she likes beer."

"That's what I was wondering," said Jesse.

Chapter 43

Sam Slocum sat in the inner sanctum of Wolf Johnson's office waiting for the town attorney to come back from court in downtown Selwin. Bonnie Griffith, Wolf's receptionist, had taken him back to the office to wait. She said Wolf had called to say court was over and he was on his way back to Conners Hill. It was less than a 15-minute drive.

Slocum had only a few minutes to wait before Johnson showed up. When Wolf appeared, he was in a good mood.

"Mornin' , Sam," he said as he walked into the cavernous office. "What brings you here today? Got some work for me?"

"Nothing like that, Wolf. I just stopped by to ask you for a word of advice. Thought you might be able to help me loosen up the mayor a little."

"Loosen him up? You know Ziglar. He's one of the least uptight people I know. If he gets any looser, he'll go flying off in all directions. I can't imagine why you'd want to loosen him up."

"Maybe that's not the right word, Wolf. What I really mean is that I'm wondering how to get him to see the positive side of the casino business. I don't think he's convinced it's a good thing for the town. In fact, he keeps telling me there are more drawbacks than advantages. I know he isn't opposed to gambling per se, but I can't seem to get him to see the positive effects a casino would have on the local economy. He's usually in favor of any business that will bring in more tax revenues and gives individual homeowners a break.. I thought maybe that since you and him are both Republicans, you'd be able to give me some suggestions as to how to go about persuading him that it's a good thing for the community."

Johnson strolled to the back of his desk, pulled the leather-bound, roll-away chair back from under the desk and sat down. He opened a silver case and took out a small wooden-tipped cigar not much bigger than a cigarette and lighted it with a lighter that matched the case. He puffed on the cigar for a moment and then laid it across a silver ash tray on the desk. He leaned back in his chair, placed both hands on the back of his head and closed his eyes. "Sam," he said, "I'm not so sure I can help you out, because I'm not sure myself that this is a good thing for the town."

"Why not?" asked the irrepressible Slocum. "I thought you were always in favor of a good business deal, and I'm sure you can see just how good the casino business is."

"Oh, I have no doubt that casinos are a good business," said Johnson. "I'm just not sure they are a good business for a small town like Conners Hill."

"But, Wolf, surely you can see that it's not just Conners Hill I'm interested in. It's the whole state. I mean casinos could be a boon to every town in the North Carolina, the same way tobacco used to be a boon to the state. And God knows, we need something like that to make up for the decline in the tobacco business. Besides probably more than half the revenue would come from out of state, from the tourist trade and the New York to Florida travelers. Naturally there are some hazards involved in gambling, but they aren't anywhere near as life-threatening or as serious as smoking tobacco. We all know that smoking can kill you. Seldom, if ever, has anyone died from gambling. Surely, that's as plain as the nose on your face."

Johnson winced at the mention of his nose. It wasn't that he was concerned about his olfactory organ, which was neither misshapen nor disproportionate for his face; it was just that he didn't like references to any part of his physical anatomy. Perhaps it was a male phobia stemming from a suspicion that one was in some way less than manly, or in some way physically incomplete. It was as irrational as the female fear that one who is not thin is fat. Most women tended always to see their bodies as something other than normal. Men could be just as irrational when it came to their physical appearance.

"Well, Sam, here's the deal. It's not gambling that Robert is opposed to. It's the idea that someone can get something for nothing. That is, Ziglar's an old-fashioned believer in cause and effect, that for every action there is a reaction.

If I know anything about him I know he believes work and effort are the prime causes of human progress, of both physical and moral health. Without them there is no financial success, no ultimate reward. You know the old expression, 'no pain, no gain'. It's a simple formula, but it's one that has been developed over eons of human existence."

"But surely the mayor is aware that there have always been exceptions to the rules, that there is such a thing as luck, or serendipity if you will. That some people succeed without trying. Some are destined to become something just because they were born, because they are here, because they fell out of the right womb."

"Of course," said Johnson "But, as a conservative, Robert believes the right heritage comes from those who worked to make it their heritage, from the rounds of blood, sweat and tears that were spilled in order for a family to get to step up the ladder in society. He believes the poor shall inherit the earth but that the rich enjoy the fruits of the earth, especially if they earned them. Naturally, there are people who have never toiled a day in their lives for what they have, but then they don't really have anything they can call their own, do they? They have the security of money and power and fame but little confidence that it is really theirs because they have paid nothing for it. It fell upon them like manna from the sky. Manna is a wonderful thing when you're hungry, but when you are full, it loses its flavor. It becomes just another mouthful, another lump in the throat of one who is already gorged with food."

"So Wolf, you are telling me that Ziglar will oppose the casinos based on his belief that a life lived without toil is not a good life, that in order to be successful one must shed blood, sweat and tears and be miserable? Is that it? Why not just tell me to go out and shoot myself?"

"Oh, I'm not saying that Robert can't be persuaded. If there's anything else about him that's certain, it's that he has an open mind. That is, he will listen to any argument that's logical and provable in a practical way. But I think his belief is that gambling is based on a rationale not unlike religion and that its value is more psychological than real. He believes the winners in life are those that make it work, not those who believe it will work if they just believe."

"So Wolf, what do I need to do to prove to the mayor and a few others around here that gambling is a practical way to benefit the town, that overall, it would be a boon, not a boondoggle?" Slocum asked.

"I have no idea," said Wolf.

"Then I guess I'll have to come up with one," said Slocum.

"I guess so, Sam," Johnson replied.

When he left the attorney's office, Slocum knew what he needed to do. He turned on to West Mountain Street and headed for Lawrence Cameron's trucking company. He and Lawrence had done business before and they could do business again. And Cameron, at least, was no ideological moralist. If he thought something would make money quickly, he would jump at the opportunity regardless of the consequences.

"Larry has always been there when I needed him," he muttered to himself. "I know I can count on him no matter what."

Chapter 44

Slocum reached Cameron's office minutes later. When he entered the small brick building surrounded by tractor-trailers, he spoke briefly to the receptionist, Sherry Devon, who ushered him back to the office without hesitation. "It's been a while since we've seen you," she said. "You used to drop by more often."

"If I'd known you were here, I wouldn't have waited so long," said Sam, recalling that Devon had worked for several local businessmen and that it was rumored she had many of the same qualities as Vivian Blaine . She was slim, blond and extremely attractive. Her smile was as inviting as the smooth, silky tone of her voice. She spoke almost in whispers but her words were clear and firm, her enunciation as fully rounded as her ample breasts.

"My God, how does Larry do it?" Sam wondered as he followed the supple figure through the hall to the company president's inner sanctum. His question was answered as soon as he entered the office. Cameron was no less particular about his surroundings than he was about his appearance and that of his female employees.

Cameron, like everyone he admired, was trim and well groomed. His office was as organized and immaculate as his tailor-made clothes. His smile was infectious. The little upward curl at the corners of his thin lips made him appear as if he'd just tasted something sweet and delicious. His face was angular and well-shaved and his jaw, while not that of a rugged athlete, was strong. His chin was not square but came to a point like the pinnacle of a pyramid turned upside down.

He rose from his chair and walked around his desk with his hand outstretched as soon as Sam entered the room. "Greetings, Sam. What brings you here this morning?" He said as he took back his hand. "You haven't paid me a visit in quite a while. I thought maybe I'd upset you or something."

"Hell, Larry, you know me better than that. I only come to you when I've got a problem and need somebody to commiserate with me. You always seem to know how to cheer me up."

"Sam, you're the last person in the world I expect to need cheering up. You're always sitting on top of the world. There's no up when you're there. The only thing to see from there is down, and I don't think you like to look down very often."

"You're right, Larry. I just need some assurance that what I'm trying to project in the empty space above me isn't some half-assed, cockamamie scheme that will cause me to fall off my perch. But I do need a little help. I need someone to assure me that my casino project isn't some wild-eyed, screwball dream—which naturally, I don't believe it is—but more than that I need someone to help me persuade some of the do-good leaders around here that it's a good thing for them and the town."

"And you came to me for help? Sam, you may be barking up the wrong tree. I'm not exactly the top of the heap when it comes to politics. Business is business, but politics is another animal altogether. The two don't always work together, though we both know they can when we play our cards right."

"Or when we have the right cards to play?" Sam interjected.

"Yeah, that, too. But what are you suggesting, Sam? Do you think you don't have the right cards or that you aren't playing them right?"

"Well, it could be a little of both. But actually, I think I've done my homework fairly well, and I think the cards I'm holding aren't too bad. I'm just not sure which ones I need to play to convince Robert Ziglar and a few others that we all win if we get into the casino business together. It's an up-and-coming legitimate enterprise, and the way the country is going, there's going to be no stopping it. We just need to catch the wave and ride it."

"You're mixing your metaphors a little, aren't you, Sam?"

"Jeez, Larry, when did you become so concerned about language? You understand what I'm talking about, don't you? Since when did mixed metaphors become a business problem?"

"Okay, Sam, but you know how important language can be. Let's start there with the problem at hand."

"What do you mean?"

"First of all, I think you should stop thinking in terms of cards and stick to waves. Cards have a bad connotation, too much association with gambling. In fact the two probably go back to the earliest days of gambling. So instead of playing your cards right, maybe you should talk to the mayor and the other do-gooders in terms of something like waves. After all, everybody loves the ocean and everybody knows that waves are as predictable as phases of the moon. There's nothing sinister about them. Unlike cards, they're part of God's creation; they just are, and most of us like them, so I suggest we talk about catching waves."

"What do you mean?"

"What I'm suggesting is that life itself is a conversation. Every social and technological trend starts with a conversation. It's a biblical thing, you know. 'In the beginning was the word....' Creating what you want in life is a matter of creating an image of it and then coming up with the words to describe it to others in such a way that it becomes desirable to them. Take almost any social trend and trace its history and you will find that it started with an idea and then with a conversation about the idea. The trends in fashion are a perfect example. Clothing, for instance. For centuries men wore clothes that made them more maneuverable; women wore clothes that hid their bodies without diminishing their femininity—long, flowing dresses, tight waists and necklines that, depending upon the era, were either high or low. As times changed and women began to act more like men by riding horses, driving cars, et cetera, ideas of what their clothing should be also changed. Today's pant suits are a result of the fact that women don't stay home most of the time. They go to work just like men, they travel like men, they see themselves more like men every day. Look at Hillary Clinton, for God's sake."

"Okay, but what's your point?"

"Well, at some point the conversation about what is fashionable changes. Women talk and they talk about the clothes they wear, about what is practical or what is fashionable. When the practical and the fashionable coincide, a new trend begins, a new era begins. It ends when something happens to cause the conversation to change. Someone comes up with a new idea and someone else begins a conversation that the new idea is a better or more practical way of doing things. If the conversation catches on, the subject of it becomes the new trend."

"So?"

"So the conversation about gambling has always been equivocal, or two-sided. There was the positive side, the side that said you could raise money for progressive things by giving people what they want in the process. In other words, raise money for building roads or schools by letting people play a game of roulette or join in a lottery. The negative side has been that some people will play the game without having the money for other things, like paying the rent or feeding their kids. It's that side of gambling that in the past has gotten the most attention because it's the most graphic. People don't like the idea of kids going without food or families being evicted for not paying their rent.

But in today's society, the conversation about gambling is changing. In America, people seldom see the real downside of poverty. The prevailing image is that the large majority of Americans are doing pretty well, and even if they are on the lower side of the economic scale, they are better off than ninety percent of the people in the rest of the world.

"And?"

"It seems to me that what you need to do is just what you've been doing to promote the conversation that gambling is no longer an evil empire run by gangsters. You need to promote it as a legitimate business that can benefit everybody. But you need a more progressive spin."

"And just how do I create that spin?"

" I'm suggesting that you keep the emphasis on the inevitability of gambling, only that you don't call it gambling. You call it the gaming industry. It sounds a lot better and it's a lot less threatening. We don't want to teach our children to gamble, but we want them to play games. Games are fun and they're healthy. Besides that, in today's world, if you include athletic competition and computer simulations, the gaming industry is a multi-billion dollar business."

"How would you suggest we turn gambling into gaming?"

"The big casinos already do it to some extent by letting more people win, by not being so greedy as to make themselves the only winners. For instance, in the slot machine sections of most big casinos, people are constantly winning. Play a machine that takes nickels and before you run through a dollar, you'll probably win a dollar or more.

Once you've become a winner and have caught the thrill of the game, you don't stop. It's like sex. Once you've had sex, you don't stop. Eventually, you come to the conclusion that what you're doing at the casino is not gambling but gaming, that you are not there to strike it rich, you're there just to have fun. And the fact is that to most casual gamblers, it is fun."

"So what do you think we should do to enforce the idea that casino gambling is a healthy game? How do we overcome the puritanical notion that it's evil?"

"We keep reinforcing the practical business aspect of the industry as well as the positive side effects. Keep reminding the public officials of the tax revenues that will come from the games. After all, it's not only the casino that will pay taxes but everyone who wins at the gaming tables. The IRS keeps tabs on the players as well as the game providers. It's a win-win situation all the way around. In fact, there's no doubt in my mind that the public revenue aspect of gambling is the only way you're going to convince Ziglar and other skeptics. And keep reminding them that today's gaming industry is a tightly regulated, legal business operation. The Mafia doesn't control the big games any longer; the government does."

"Larry, I know I can always count on you for good advice. Not only have you cheered me up, you've helped convince me that what I'm trying to do is the right thing. I've always been sure that even if gambling has some negative aspects, it's not a criminal activity. It's providing a little excitement to people who might not have much else in their lives. But I've got one other problem, however.

How do I get to the two or three dyed-in-the-wool skeptics who are just flat-out opposed to the idea of gambling?"

"Where they are concerned, you might have to use something a little more aggressive."

"Like what?"

"Perhaps a simple trap with some irresistible bait."

"Such as?"

"Such as the thing most men can't or won't refuse."

"You mean sex.?"

"What else would I have in mind."

"What else is there?"

CHAPTER 45

Cee informed Vivian that he had let someone know where she was. "They will come to pick you up any time now," he told her. "In the meantime, explain to me how you came to be here in the first place."

"I thought you didn't like explanations."

"I don't, but sometimes they make sense."

"Well, this one probably won't."

"Why not?"

"Because there's no sense to it."

"How so?"

"It's like this: I had an argument with a woman who thinks I'm trying to destroy her husband's business. Nothing could be further from the truth, but she thinks it's so and there's no convincing her otherwise."

"What does her husband do?"

"He's a banker."

Perfect Imperfection

"How could you destroy a banker's business?"
"By convincing people that he's crooked."
"And how would you do that?"
"By convincing them he does business with crooked people."
"You mean like Mafia people?
"Maybe, or people like them."
"How do you know he does business with these people?"
"I do some business with them, too."
"What kind of business?"
"I'd rather not say."
"Why not?"
"It's private?"
"You mean you're ashamed of it?"
"Yeah."
"Then why do you do it?"
"I don't know."
"When did you start doing business with them?"
"About five years ago."
"Why?"
"Why what?"
"Why did you start doing business with them."
"My marriage wasn't working."
"Why not?"
"I don't know. It just wasn't."
"Did your husband mistreat you?"
"No."
"Did he ignore you?"
"No."
"Was he unfaithful?"

"No."
"So what was the problem?"
"He was too good for me."
"How so?"
"He treated me like a princess."
"And that's a bad thing?"
"Perhaps for me."
"Why is that?"
"I don't deserve it?"
"Why not?"
"I'm a slut."
"Who says?"
"I do."
"Why?"
"I don't know. Why is anyone what they are?"
"When did you become a slut?"
"When I was eighteen."
"What did you do?"
"I slept with my boyfriend."
"And that made you a slut?"
"According to my mother."
"What about your father?"
"He had a full time slut?"
"Did you love your father?"
"Of course."
"Did he betray you with the other woman?"

Vivian looked at Cee as if he had struck her in the face with the back of his hand. The pain was not so much from the blow as from the spasm of recognition that shot through her entire body. For the first time in her life, she realized it was not her mother's anger at her father that had controlled her life—it was her own anger at her father for having an affair with another woman. He had not only betrayed her mother, he had betrayed her. It was as if she had been rejected by the only man she really loved. He had wounded her mother's pride, but he had killed any love Vivian had ever felt for him. She looked at Cee as if he had been her father and she wanted to strike out at him as well, but she could not move. She was wracked with the pain of discovering the real cause of her misery and of her desire to destroy as many men as possible. They were all liars and cheats and they needed to be punished for their infidelities. And, as she had decided years earlier to punish them one by one, she realized now that she had been punishing herself for having been deceived by them. She had vowed to get even with men even if it meant destroying herself in the process.

Despite having recognized her quandary, Vivian Blaine could see no way out other than carrying through her plan to wreak havoc on every influential man in Conner's Hill.

Chapter 46

At the Conners Hill News, Jesse Stallings was making a phone call to Ernie Blaine. He tried Blaine's office first, then his home. On the third ring, a woman answered. Jesse was surprised but relieved when she explained that she was Ernie's sister. She had been looking after the Blaine children every afternoon after school. Jesse told her who he was and that he was trying to reach Ernie because he had some good news.

"Is it news about Vivian?" the sister asked.

"It is," said Jesse. "We think we know where she is and we believe she's all right."

"That's too bad," said the sister. "Whatever happened to her, she had it coming. She's driven my brother crazy for the last few years. I don't know how he's put up with her this long."

Perfect Imperfection

"I'm sorry to hear that," said Jesse, "but at least now Ernie will know the mother of his children is not missing. Perhaps the two of them can begin to make amends. Sometimes it takes something drastic to begin a change in the way we behave."

"Yeah, I guess that's so, but Ernie's been through more than any man deserves to bear. I have my problems with him sometimes, but he's a good man. He doesn't deserve to have to put up with a woman like Vivian."

"Well, I just wanted to let Ernie know she will probably be back soon. Maybe they can work things out."

"Maybe."

The discussion at Cee's was taking a different turn at the moment. Despite his usual indifference to matters of human emotions and actions, Cee was genuinely curious as to how Vivian came to be battered and bruised and left in the woods, perhaps to die. He pursued the issue hesitantly but with determination.

"What brought you out here to the lake?" he asked her.

"I came for a walk with a female acquaintance," Vivian replied.

"What happened to the acquaintance?"

"I don't know."

"Does she live near here."

"I don't know exactly where here is."

"We're a hundred yards or so up the hill from the lake."

"Then she lives near here."

"Who is this she you're referring to?"

"Nan Seemore."

"The banker's wife?"

"That's the one."
"Are you good friends?"
"Not really."
"Is she an enemy?"
"No."
"So what was the last thing you remember before you woke up here in my place?"
"Nan and I were talking about a mutual acquaintance."
"Who was the acquaintance?"
"Lawrence Cameron."
"The trucking company owner?"
"Yes."
"What was the discussion about?"
"About the fact that we both like him."
"Is that what brought you out to the lake?"
"What do you mean?"
"I mean did you come to the lake to talk about Cameron?"
"Yes."
"Why?"
"We had had some disagreement during a dinner at Out West and I wanted to clear the air."
"What was the disagreement?"
"Nan thought I had been fooling around with Larry and she didn't like it."
"Why?"
"She had a mid-life crush on him?"
"Had the two of you been fooling around?"
"Who?"
"You and Larry."
"A little?"

"Why?"

"Because he is a good-looking man and very smooth. I once worked for him. He was a good boss. He helped me get my priorities straight."

"How so?"

"He told me how I could use my talents to gather information and make some money in the process. He said all kinds of businessmen need information, especially bankers and lawyers and the like."

"Did you need the money?"

"Not really. I was more interested in the information."

"Why?"

"For personal reasons."

"What did you do with the information when you got it?"

"I filed it away."

"You mean you wrote it down in notebooks or something?"

"Or something."

"How else did you keep it."

"Tape recordings."

"Why tape recordings?"

"I knew that whatever I wrote down could be contested in court. It would be my word against theirs. I was mostly a nobody in this town when I came here and nobody would believe what I had to say in case it came down to my word or theirs. Besides, much of what I had was very intimate stuff. It would make a good tell-all novel."

"Do you plan to write a novel?"

"Perhaps."

"Where did you keep these records?"

"At Larry's office."
"Were they accessible to him?"
"Yes."
"Did you expect him to use some of the information for his own purposes?"
"Sure."
"Why?"
"He was paying me for it."
"So you were still working for him."
"Yeah, I guess so.."
"Didn't you ever feel you were being used?"
"Sometimes."
"Did you ever wonder if Larry would betray you?"
"Not much?"
"Why not?"
"Because I had some tapes of him and me."
"And they weren't among the ones you left at his office?
"You got it."

CHAPTER 47

"Vivian, I have one other question," said Cee Edmunds.
"What is it?" asked Vivian.
"Who hit you and why?"
"I don't know."
"You have no idea?"
"No."
"What was the last thing you remember before waking up?"
"Nan and I were walking through the woods to the trail around the lake."
"Why?"
"I had a six-pack of beer, and she and I decided to walk through the woods and drink it while we walked."
"Why?"
"Because we both like beer."

"No. What I mean is: why did you walk through the woods with it?"

"Nan's husband is a teetotaler. He doesn't like it when she drinks and he particularly doesn't like it when she drinks beer."

"Why's that?"

"He thinks beer-drinking isn't refined. He thinks he's above that sort of thing and that his wife should be, too. Besides that, he doesn't like me."

"Why not?"

"He says I'm a slut and any respectable person wouldn't be seen with me."

"What makes him think you're a slut?"

"I remind him of his mother."

"Do you think his mother drank beer?"

"Probably."

"Do you think his mother was a loose woman?"

"I have no idea, but probably so."

"Why?"

"I remind him of her."

"How did he come to that opinion of you?"

"He likes women who like sex."

"So you're saying that in public Josh Seemore hates wanton women but that in private he likes them?"

"Yeah."

"Could he have been the one who hit you while you and Nan were walking?"

"I don't think so."

"Why not?"

"Nan said he was at a meeting at Sam Slocums."

"Then who do you think it could have been?"

"Anybody."

Edmunds was about to give up on the idea of finding out who had slipped up behind Vivian, knocked her out and then kicked her several times while she lay on the ground, but he had one more question.

"Vivian, who else could have possibly known that you and Nan were out walking in the woods that evening?"

"The only one I can imagine would be Bebe Bullis."

"How's that?"

"Nan said she told Bebe where she was going when she left the restaurant. She said Bebe followed her to the restroom before she left and Nan asked her if she wanted to join us at the lake. Bebe likes Nan and I think she likes me as well."

"If that's so, why would she want to do you any harm?"

"I have a tape of her husband and me."

"Does she know that?"

"I don't know."

"Then what motive would she have had for attacking you?"

"I don't know. Maybe she thinks Nan and I had something going ."

"You mean she might have been jealous of you and Nan being together?"

"Possibly."

"Why do you think that?"

"Well, it seems that wherever Nan goes or whatever she does, Bebe is always there at her side."

"Isn't that true of a lot of good friends?"

"Of course, but I think it may be more than just friendship."

"How's that?"

"Nan has money and a high-class background and Bebe has neither. Nan is prominent in Conners Hill social circles and Bebe isn't. Nan has an outgoing personality and Bebe is rather quiet and introverted."

"So you're saying their relationship is a physical one in that opposites attract?"

"Something like that."

"Do you think there was anything physical going on between Nan and Bebe?"

"Maybe."

"Why?"

"Because Nan is bi-sexual."

"How do you know that?"

"Jonah told me."

"And why did you ask him something like that?"

"Because Nan is always attacking the gay community as if gays are the lowest form of humanity, and people who attack others too openly are often trying to draw attention away from themselves. I mean look at you. People ridicule you and call you an idiot because they want other people to believe they are not like you. But the truth, as I see it, is that most of us despise the things we most fear is a part of ourselves. You want people to think that you despise words and idle talk because it is misleading and unnecessary, when in reality you love words and find them as alluring as sex itself. You wear the mask of hypocrisy the same as everybody else, but no doubt you hide behind the mask out of fear."

"And what fear would that be?"

"That you are not a good talker."

"You have a point, but my fear is based on fact."
"What fact?"
"I'm not a good talker."
"Then what the hell have we been doing here for the last half hour?"
"Good question."

Chapter 48

Back at the Conners Hill News, Jesse Stallings and Dave Devlin were beginning to fit the pieces of Vivian's disappearance together. Janice had discovered during a conversation with several other Garden Club members that Bebe Bullis left the dinner meeting shortly after Nan Seemore. She told the other women she had a headache and was going home to take a couple of aspirin and go to bed.

Jesse had called Chief Grady to tell him he believed Vivian was alive and well and at Cee Edmunds' lake cabin. Grady wanted to know how Jesse came by his information. Jesse told him Cee had given him a message.

"Cee talked to you?" the chief asked.

"Chief, you know Cee doesn't talk much to anybody. He wrote me a cryptic note, but I'm sure it was about Vivian."

"Why, what did it say?"

"He just said, 'She's with me'."

"That's it?"

"Yeah, but I'm sure it is about Vivian. Cee and I ate breakfast together several days ago and I happened to mention her disappearance. He didn't say anything at the time, but I noticed he seemed a little nervous when I mentioned her name. I may be wrong, but I think you should send someone out to Cee's place to check it out."

"Okay, Jesse. I'll let you know what they find."

"Thanks, Chief."

Meanwhile, Cee and Vivian continued their conversation about hiding one's deepest feelings behind the masks of opposition. Cee had admitted that his fascination with words had led him into a life of reading and contemplation, which in turn had led him into the study of psychology and religion, and ultimately to Zen Buddhism.

"What is it you find so interesting in Zen?" asked Vivian.

"Everything," said Cee.

"Everything?"

"Everything and nothing."

"There you go again. Isn't everything and nothing just a way of hiding one's confusion about everything?"

"Not necessarily."

"Why not?"

"Because everything is no-thing."

"In what sense?"

"In the deepest sense. In the deepest knowledge we have about everything. Take physics, for instance. What has our study of physics told us about the universe and all that's in it?"

"That it's all made of the same basic stuff: atoms and molecules and a host of even smaller stuff like protons and neutrons, electrons and such."

"On the surface we're all—man and animal, plants and trees, mountains and rivers—just coagulations of these invisible, infinitesimal bits of energy."

"So?"

"So this energy has decided to take certain forms and shapes and become whatever it is that we call ourselves and our world. When one form or shape changes, it becomes another form or shape."

"So rather than the phrase 'earth to earth and dust to dust' we should be saying 'energy to energy'? What's the difference, it's all just stuff and words about stuff."

"True, but energy constantly reformulates itself into certain patterns in the real world. Your energy may reform itself into a plant or animal or even a rock, or as a part of any of those. The ultimate question is: what determines what the new pattern will be?"

"That would be God, naturally."

"You could say that. Or you could say that it will be chance, evolution, or what have you, perhaps even your own intentions. But in the final analysis, it's going to be just another bundle of energy."

"So what's your point?"

"The point is we may or may not be able to affect what kind of bundle it will be, or when or where it will be."

"And?"

Perfect Imperfection

"And we have to just let nature take its course and be who and what we are without trying to affect the outcome."

"Again, what's the point?"

"The point is there's no point in trying to change the course of nature or to determine the outcome ourselves. We should just be with what is and let nature take its course. In other words, go with the flow."

"Isn't that sort of like saying 'Don't worry, be happy, everything will turn out the way it's supposed to?' "

"Yeah."

"What if it doesn't?"

"What if it doesn't?"

"What should we do about it?"

"Nothing."

"Okay, Cee. Here's my point. If we were all to go skipping merrily along as if we didn't have a care in the world, nothing would get done and everything would be in a mess, right?"

"Right."

"No, wrong. We have to take some action to have it turn out right."

"And what would right be?"

"Better than now."

"So we should take some action to make the world better than it is now?"

"Right."

"Vivian, what do you think man has been trying to do since the world began?"

"Make it better."

"And has the world gotten better? Did Adam improve paradise? Or are we now in a world more dangerous and more chaotic than ever before? Oh, we have more material goods today, more things, in other words more stuff, and many of us live as if our lives were better. But is the world better? Have we not polluted everything in our world, including our rivers and oceans, our air and even our minds? Have we made the world safer for ourselves or our children? If we are honest, I think we would have to say no."

"Perhaps you're right."

Chapter 49

An hour later, a black unmarked police car pulled up in front of Cee Edmunds' cabin. Sgt. Alan Malloy got out and headed toward the front entrance. When Malloy knocked on the cabin door, Cee peered through a crack, saw who was there and then opened it wide to let in the policeman.

Instead of entering, Malloy remained on the front stoop.

"Mr. Edmunds, I believe you have a young woman here who's been missing. Is that correct?"

"Yes," said Cee.

"Good, then we have come to take her back."

" Back where?"

"Where she belongs."

"And that would be?"

"To town, to her friends and associates."

"What about her family?"

"Yeah, that too."

"Do you know Mrs. Blaine well, Sergeant?"

"Well enough?"

"What does that mean?"

"I know her well enough to know she's in a lot of trouble."

"Really?"

"It really isn't any of your business, is it, Edmunds?"

"Depends."

"On what?"

"On what you have in mind."

"Edmunds, I can assure you that we have Mrs. Blaine's best interests in mind."

"What are we so interested in?"

"Her interests in the development and progress of Conners Hill. We want to keep her on track."

"What track is that?"

"The right one, of course."

"I see."

"I doubt that you do, but just to make it clear, Vivian...excuse me, Mrs. Blaine...has played a significant role in helping convince some businessmen to take a more positive position toward the town's future recreation plans."

"How did she do that?"

"Edmunds, it really isn't any of your business, so would you please just call Mrs. Blaine and let us get on with our job."

"Okay," said Cee. "You may come in and wait for her if you like."

"That won't be necessary. Just have her come out and we'll take care of everything from here on."

Cee looked to the patrol car parked just twenty feet from his front door. He saw two men he didn't recognize in the car, both in the back seat. They both wore baseball caps with the bills pulled down to shield their eyes. They held their heads down and their hands up to their faces.

"Is Vivian's husband with you?" Cee asked Malloy.

"That's none of your concern," the sergeant replied.

Before Cee could say anything else, Vivian stepped out from behind him onto the stoop.

"Hi, Alan," she said, smiling at Malloy. "I suppose you've come to take me home."

"Sure," said Sgt. Malloy, "there's a lot of people who want you back."

Vivian walked toward the waiting car. Malloy opened the door to the back seat. One of the men got out. He ushered Vivian inside. Before she was in, she recognized the man in the back and started to pull back. He grabbed her wrist and pulled her into the car. He clasped his arm around her waist and his hand over her mouth.

Cee had followed Vivian to the car. "What's going on?" he said to Malloy.

"I told you it's none of your concern, but if you must know we're taking Mrs. Blaine down to headquarters to ask her a few questions. That's all."

"Why are you treating her as if she's a criminal?"

"Who said we are?"

"I did. Looks as if she's being forced to go with you."

"She got into the car of her own accord, Edmunds. I wouldn't bother myself with her further if I were you."

"But you aren't me."

"Look, Edmunds, don't be so nosy. Everybody knows you're the town idiot and if anything else happens to this woman, most people will believe you did it. They'll think you beat her up and held her a prisoner out here."

"You think she's been beaten?"

"Isn't it obvious. She's a beautiful woman. I've never seen her look so bad."

"Perhaps she's sick."

"Oh, she's sick all right."

"How would you know?"

"I know. I know a damn sight more about her than you do, I think."

Edmunds realized he was powerless to stop the policeman from taking Vivian away, but he wasn't without some resources. As soon as the police car pulled out of the driveway, he left the cabin by the back door and walked swiftly through the woods to the park attendant's office just above the boat docks.

"May I use your phone?" he asked the attendant.

"Sure, just don't stay on it too long."

Cee dialed the number of the Conners Hill Police Department. When the dispatcher answered, Cee asked abruptly, "Did you send a patrol car to my house a while ago?"

"Who are you?" said the dispatcher.

"I'm Cee Edmunds."

"Well, if we did I don't know anything about it," the dispatcher responded.

"Who would know?" asked Cee.

"Maybe the chief or one of the captains."

"Is the chief there?'

"Yeah, I'll connect you."

Stanfield Grady picked up the phone on his desk. "This is the chief. Can I help you?"

"Stan, this Cee. Did you send Alan Malloy out to my house to pick up Vivian Blaine?"

"Hi, Cee. Yeah I asked him to go get her about an hour and a half ago. Is there a problem?'

"Who were the two men you sent with Malloy? I didn't recognize them."

"I don't know," said the chief. "I told Malloy to pick up Mrs. Blaine because I had gotten a tip she was at your place. I didn't tell him to take anyone with him."

"Well, there were two men with him when they came to my place. It looked like one of them pulled Vivian into the back seat against her will. Malloy said they were bringing her to the police station for questioning."

"That's funny," said the chief. "I told Malloy to take her straight home from your place. I didn't instruct him to question her."

"Well, Chief, maybe you need to find out what's going on."

"Believe me, Cee, I will. I certainly will."

Chapter 50

Vivian had ceased to struggle with the men in the back seat of the squad car. Once they reached Valley School Road, Malloy turned left and headed toward Watertown.

"Where are we going?" asked Vivian. "This isn't the way to my house."

"It is if you want it to be," Malloy responded.

"What is that supposed to mean?"

"It means if you cooperate, we'll take you home. If you don't, we won't."

"Alan, what the hell are you up to?" Vivian shouted. "I thought we were friends."

"Oh, we're friends, all right. I just thought I might find out just how good a friend you are."

A mile or so later, Malloy slowed down, made a right turn onto a narrow dirt road leading through a patch of dense woods and came to a stop in front of an old tobacco barn at the end of the road. A small gray compact car was parked beside the barn. Malloy got out of the squad car, opened the left rear door and signaled for Vivian to get out and follow him. The other two men stayed in the car.

Inside the dirt-floored barn a single dim light bulb hung on a cord from the ceiling. It produced just enough light for Vivian to see two men step from behind the door . One of the men she didn't know, but the other she recognized immediately.

"Vincent," Vivian muttered. "What are you doing here?"

"Protecting my interests," Vincent Sigman replied.

"Oh, and what might they be?"

"You and my investments," he answered.

"What do I have to do with your investments?"

"I think you know that already."

"Actually, I don't have a clue. Please fill me in."

"Vivian, you know I've been working with Sam Slocum on his project to bring casino gambling to the state."

"Yeah, that much I know."

"Then you should know that I've been trying to help him line up support for the project among the town's leaders."

"I could have figured that out if I hadn't already. So where do I fit into all this?"

"You have some information about some town officials that we think might be useful."

"I don't know what you're talking about."

"Oh, come now, Vivian, you're not that naive. We know you have some personal information about several of these men. We just want to make sure you use that information wisely—in a way that has a positive effect on the community."

"And positive in your mind means what exactly, Vincent?"

"Positive means doing what's best for the people of the town. Positive means bringing the gaming industry here in order to raise the standard of living for everybody concerned, businesses as well as taxpayers."

"What's in it for me?" Vivian asked.

"You get to exert a powerful influence in the community. You get the satisfaction of knowing that what you do and say is important, that you are a force to be reckoned with, or, putting it a little less subtly perhaps, that you are the queen bee in this neck of the woods."

"So what do I have to do to achieve this so-called queen bee status, Vincent, screw every worker in the hive?"

"Of course not, Vivian. As I understand it, you've laid most of the groundwork already. I mean we pretty much know how you came by the information we need. All we want you to do is to let certain of these leaders know that you have the information and that it's in their best interests to make sure you don't make it public."

"I've never been interested in making it public," said Vivian. "It wouldn't be good for me or them. The only thing I'm interested in is their knowing what kind of hypocrites they are and that if any one of them gets really out of line, I'm here to call them on it. Alan, should know. I'm kind of like a cop who can arrest most anybody at any time but doesn't because his real job is merely to make people aware that he can."

"So I presume you are willing to take on a leadership role and make sure we bring a few of the anti-gaming businessmen into the fold.?"

"I didn't say that," said Vivian.

"Then what did you say?"

"I didn't say anything."

"For crying out loud, Vivian, Alan Malloy shouted. "You sound just like Cee Edmunds. He hasn't fucked up your mind, has he?"

"No, Alan. He hasn't fucked with my mind, but during the past week he has enabled me to see a lot of things more clearly."

"Such as?"

"Such as the fact that people seldom say what they mean or mean what they say. They're usually more interested in getting what they want when they want it. Just like Vincent, here. He says he wants to improve the community when what he really wants is to make a mint from the casinos, and the community be damned. Once he's made his money, he'll high-tail it back to New York and the locals will be left to sort out the problems he helped create. It's no different than what most big businessmen do if they have the money and the power. What these guys usually say is they want to help the town grow, and for the most part they do, because when the town grows their businesses will grow with it, but so will a lot of problems the rest of us hadn't counted on. There'll be more people, more traffic, more crime and more taxes. And what happens when that happens? The people who made a fortune will take their money and go somewhere where there are fewer people, less traffic, less crime and fewer taxes. The yokels who bought into the high-sounding bullshit will be left to clean up the mess. Isn't that right, Vincent."

"Some of it, perhaps, but not all. It depends on the leaders and those who support them. Take Mayor Ziglar, for instance. Do you really think he would pull up stakes and leave Conners Hill? He loves the town and its people more than he loves power or money. Oh, yeah, power and money are important to him, but I don't see him abandoning the town or doing anything that would destroy the pride or dignity of the people who live in it. After all, they are the ultimate source of his power and his money. Without them, he would be just another small fish in a very big pond."

"OK, so maybe you're right about Ziglar, Vincent, but surely you won't deny that your primary interest in the town is what you can take from it, will you? That's what you're here for, isn't it? When you've got what you want you'll leave Conners Hill and go back to your high society women and begin playing the investment game somewhere else. Isn't that right?"

"Maybe but maybe not. It's true I will not be staying in Conners Hill indefinitely, but I won't be leaving it behind either. Investments have to be looked after, otherwise they don't amount to much. And remember, I said my investments included something else besides monetary goods."

"Oh, yeah. What was that?"

"You," said Vincent. "When I go, I want to take you with me?"

"Why would you want to do that?"

"Because I've grown very fond of you."

"What does 'very fond' mean?"

"It means I have found you to be the most alluring woman I've ever met."

"That's it?"

"Well, there's a little more."

"And what's that?"

"It means I want to be with you for the rest of my life."

"That's all?"

"What else is there?"

"How about the rest of my life?"

"You get to be with me."

"Oh, brother."

Chapter 51

Vivian gave Vincent Sigman no assurances that she would use what she knew to influence the decisions of the town leaders she knew to be vulnerable to such blackmail. She said merely that she would consider it. She had, in fact, considered using her knowledge to persuade the same men not to join forces with the proponents of casino gambling. Her reasoning was not based on moral grounds, but on the simple notion that putting more money and power into the hands of dishonorable men would lead only to more abuse of the money and power and to more dishonorable acts by those who abused it. Vivian was, after all, a moralist at heart.

Nonetheless, she felt a genuine affection for many of the men whose flaws had to be weighed against the value of their moral strengths. Experience had taught her that all men and women were flawed but that most were conscientious and repentant in the face of self-knowledge. Many, if not most, understood that sin, like sex, was more a condition of humanity than a conscious choice and that perhaps the greatest sin of humanity was not the quest for money and power but the propensity to judge one another.

Cee explained the sin of judgment to her in the simplest of terms. "Judgment," he said, "is not choosing on the basis of right and wrong. It is choosing to believe that right and wrong are absolutes rather than relatives. More often than not, it is choosing to believe as absolute what you believe rather than what is indicated by the evidence.."

"What does that mean?" Vivian asked.

"It means that everything that is, is relative."

"For example?"

"Day is relative to night, dark is relative to light, good is relative to evil, God is relative to the devil. One without the other is inconceivable. They depend on each other."

"Then you are saying there is no good without evil?"

"Absolutely."

"Absolutely? Isn't that a contradiction in a world where everything is relative?"

"Yes."

"And you can live with such a contradiction?"

"Of course."

"Isn't what you say a paradox, that what is, isn't and what isn't, is?"

"Certainly."

"How can anything be absolute if it isn't what it is or it is what it isn't?"

"With relative ease."

"How so?"

"Because relativity is the absolute."

"You mean like change is the only constant?"

"Exactly."

"So when everything that exists is constantly changing, the change is the absolute."

"You got it."

"So you are saying that today I am one thing and tomorrow I will be something else?"

"Certainly."

"That's bull crap!"

"That's changing, too. Today it is bull crap, tomorrow it will be fertilizer; next year it will be corn, or potatoes. After that, it will be crap again, but a different kind of crap.."

"What about God?"

"What about Her?"

"Surely God doesn't change."

"Surely."

"So when everything else changes, God remains the same."

"Of course. As the creator, She is the creator of constant change."

"Which means what?"

"Which means nothing. Or perhaps more accurately, no-thing. That is, everything that exists, including God, is a no-thing something."

"Another paradox."

"Yes."

"Where does that leave us mere mortals?"

"Where we've always been."

"And where's that?"

"In the hands of God."

Vivian was confused by it all, and yet she was aware that something in the deepest recesses of her mind, perhaps in her very soul, had shifted. Suddenly she became aware that what had happened to her as a child, and as a child becoming a woman, was not as dramatic nor as traumatic as she had believed. What had happened was merely what had happened. It was a sequence of events in a constantly changing sequence of events in which she had become not a victim but a victimizer. Instead of reforming her father, she had become her father. She had done to Ernie exactly what her father had done to her and her mother, only she had done it to every other man she had known.

Without warning, her entire body began to tremble and shake. She fell on her hands and knees and cried out in despair. "My God, my God, what have I done? How can I ever be forgiven? How can I ever forgive myself?"

Cee stood quietly beside her, saying nothing. He knew she had become acutely aware of having lived most of her life in the shadow of her father's infidelity, that she had made it not a failure of his character but a fault of her own for having allowed it to happen. She had condemned herself to a life of disgust and despair. It was a life that, she felt instinctively, was now over. Miraculously, a hundred pound weight was gone from her shoulders. When she arose to face Cee, she was a changed woman. She could embrace an uncertain future with hope and joy. She threw her arms around Cee and hugged him tightly.

"Cee, you are the most remarkable man I have ever met. I thank you with all my heart and soul. Tell me how

I can repay you for what you have done. There is nothing I would not do for you."

"I ask nothing of you," Cee replied. "except that you be who you are, a child of God, perfection itself."

Stammering almost incoherently, Vivian hugged him again. Not fully confident of her absolution, she protested. "But how can I be a child of God when I am imperfect in every way, a total mess," she cried.

"Perfect imperfection, imperfect perfection. You are what you are, which is what God intended that you be."

"So why am I such a personal disaster?

"So that others can see what personal disaster looks like and avoid making the same mistakes."

"You are saying that God chose me to show others how not to behave."

"Of course. Just as he chose the Jews to show others how not to behave."

"What do you mean?"

"Did God choose the Jews to be his people or did the Jews choose God to be their strength and redeemer? The answer is both. The history of the Jewish people is one of continuous infidelity and redemption, the same as the rest of humanity but with one major difference."

"That being?"

"The rest of humanity did not choose to be God's chosen people. We chose imperfection over perfection, individualism and chaos over integration and unity, discord over harmony—perfect imperfection over imperfect perfection. While we give lip service to God, we are continually choosing the way of the world over God's way. We prefer envy, anger, jealousy, greed and hostility to love, peace, tranquility and stability. Even our terms for physical love are more often than not used in anger and derision. We say to the world: fuck this, screw that, suck this, suck that, kiss this, kiss that. What could be more godless than to turn natural physical love into a conversation of enmity and hate?

"I never thought of it that way," said Vivian.

"Most of us don't think that way because we are too close to ourselves. We cannot see ourselves the way others see us. We can only see images of ourselves in a mirror or a photograph. The mirror shows us a reverse image and the photograph a static image. We can get closer perhaps by looking at ourselves in a movie or a video, but even then it is two dimensional and incomplete. But how many of us like to see ourselves in a movie or video? Most of us run when someone points a camera at us. Why? Because we are afraid we might see ourselves as we really are. We are afraid our imperfections might be translated into derision and ridicule, that we might be made to feel even more imperfect than we really are."

"So, Cee, are you saying that to choose God is to choose ourselves the way we are, with all our flaws and imperfections? Isn't that blasphemous?"

"Only if you believe God's creation is blasphemous."

Chapter 52

Before Vivian returned home, she resolved to lead a totally different life from the one she had been living. Getting even with the men in her life by getting it on with them was no longer a priority. Still, she felt it was necessary not to let all of what she knew about them go to waste. Vincent's suggestion that she could put that knowledge to good use sounded more and more reasonable the longer she thought about it. He had suggested she might become a significant influence in the community and that as such she would have the power and leverage to make changes in the character of the town. She had always believed that gambling, like alcohol, was a debilitating addiction and that the less of it there was the better off society would be. But she also knew that addiction to gambling and alcohol, like sex, were human temptations that would not go away.

Perfect Imperfection

Perhaps gambling, such as that provided by a state lottery, could be a positive influence in a community where there was little else to excite the mind or stir the blood. After all, didn't the people who promoted such lotteries do so with the best of intentions. In North Carolina, the state lottery was to be used for education and nothing else. Money for burgeoning school populations was in short supply, and a lottery was a way to induce people to contribute to schools without resorting to more involuntary taxes. Playing the lottery, she knew, was a foolish thing personally, given the fact that the chances of actually winning anything substantial were extremely slim. But somebody would win, and the schools would benefit, and, most importantly, one did not have to play. One was free either to participate or not to participate. No one was forced to do anything they did not choose to do.

Nonetheless, Vivian also realized that wherever large amounts of money were involved, there was temptation and inevitable corruption. Anywhere there was a massive influx of cash, there were people hell bent on getting some of it for themselves, especially if the pipeline was privately controlled. Even if the owners were honorable and upstanding citizens, one could not always count on the dealers, the managers, the accountants or the bankers to be as upstanding and honorable. Given the opportunity, even ministers and other church officials were sometimes guilty of succumbing to temptation.

Vivian was dead set against any organization that was large enough to hire lawyers and accountants to manage large sums of money. She had heard the arguments made by Sam Slocum and others about how modern casinos were run by accountants and lawyers and regulated by government, but she wasn't buying the notion that government regulation was a failsafe preventative of corruption and fraud. The federal government itself was continuously looted by charlatans and thieves posing as public servants inside the halls of Congress.

In an odd sort of way, Vivian considered herself a moralist, one who understood right and wrong and had chosen to do what was right. But in her personal life she had chosen to do right in the wrong way. She had chosen to make men pay, and to pay dearly, for their sins. She had chosen to teach them a hard lesson, the lesson that all actions, good and bad, have inevitable consequences, and that sometimes the consequences of doing good could turn out badly. Most all nations went to war for what their leaders considered good intentions. Those good intentions often led to bad consequences. In the end every intention and every action was a two-edged sword capable of slicing up the thing it was wielded to protect.

Vivian reasoned that not acting at all sometimes had consequences as bad or worse than wrong action. Not choosing to do right was a way of choosing to do wrong. Standing by while someone was raped or murdered was tantamount to participating in the crime itself; it was unforgivable. Better to be killed than to participate in a killing by doing nothing to prevent it. Vivian decided, therefore, to do what she believed was right.

She decided to carry out the plan she had devised the day she and Ernie had moved to Conners Hill. She didn't know exactly what to do, but she knew that it could be done. Once she had made up her mind, once the will was there, the means would somehow be made known to her. Perhaps Cee could help. In the meantime, Vivian would have to make amends with Ernie and his family. She knew it would not be easy, but it would be the only way she could keep her children and continue to live in Conners Hill with any degree of respect. It was going to be more difficult than she imagined.

Chapter 53

"We have nothing to worry about," Vincent Sigman reported to Sam Slocum. "Vivian is on our side and given what she knows about those who oppose our plans, there's no reason to believe they will not come around to our point of view very quickly. I will help her with some of the details, but all I can say at the moment is that Vivian will be able to use what she knows to change some hearts and minds in a flash."

Slocum nodded, smiling. He leaned back in his swivel chair and placed the tips of the fingers of his hands together as if in a gesture of a prayer of thanksgiving. "You've done well, Vincent, but are you certain we can count on Vivian? A past like hers must have pitfalls. Have you checked her out thoroughly enough to know what her ultimate motivations are and whether they can be used to our advantage?"

"I've had our people do an extensive background check on her, Sam. I can give you her life's history, where she comes from, who her parents were, what her life was like growing up in a small town in eastern North Carolina, whom she dated in high school and college and how she came to marry Ernie Blaine and settle down in Conners Hill, if you can call it settling down."

"That's what I mean," said Sam. "Someone as seemingly unsettled as Vivian could end up being a problem. Do you think we can count on her when the chips are down, or is she likely to change directions on the spur of the moment? Personally, I like Vivian and believe she has many admirable qualities, but I haven't been around her enough to know whether she's all that she appears to be. I guess what I'm driving at is whether or not she's mentally stable or a loaded gun ready to go off at the slightest jar."

"Sam, you and I both know that one can never know everything about anyone other than one's self and that more often than not we don't even know ourselves very well. But from what I've been able to determine, Vivian is as stable as a woman can be given that she's a woman. Despite some problems with her early home life and, from what I've been able to gather, a mother and father who really didn't get along very well, Vivian has a solid background. She was a top student in high school and college, and, from what I've learned from those she's worked for here, she's a quick learner and a hard worker who is reliable and dependable. She's been married to Ernie for ten years, and as far as we know, most of those years were fairly stable. The only problems I've been able to find are the obvious ones. She likes to drink a little too much and she likes men who make a difference. Other than that, I'd call her a first-class citizen."

"Okay, Vincent, I'm going to take your word for it. I think you know your business, and if you think Vivian is someone we can rely on, then it's settled. Help her in any way you can and let's get this show out of rehearsals and into the spotlight. I want to present our proposal for casino gambling to the state legislature as soon as the spring session begins. By then, we need to have all our ducks in a row and our guns loaded. But we don't want any misfires between now and then. Can we count on that?"

"Absolutely, Sam. A year from now we should be ready for business."

"That's all I want to know. Just keep me informed as to how it's going."

Vincent left Sam's office satisfied that his plan was as good as anyone could devise. He had not mentioned to Sam that he believed Vivian might suffer from a psychological condition that could be a problem. Nonetheless, he suspected that Vivian's fondness for men was definitely psychological and that she harbored some kind of deep resentment that went far beyond the mere desire to manipulate or control them. He had begun to suspect it when he learned from his sources that Vivian's mother and father had maintained little more than the illusion of a solid marriage and that Vivian's own marriage to Ernie Blaine was not that dissimilar. The apple doesn't fall far from the tree, he thought. It was a cliche', but what was a cliché other than a statement that was so true it had lasted for centuries, even for millennium. Modern religion was sustained and strengthened by such clichés. Love itself was a cliché that no one could deny.

Vincent's only problem with Vivian was that he himself had become smitten by her. He had never even held her hand, but he was hopelessly in love with her. Every time she looked at him the blood rushed to his head and his face began to redden. In her presence, he was a helpless child. His mind turned into a quivering jelly and his heart pounded against his chest like a hammer against a giant bell, each ring sending echoes of desire through his entire body. Not until he was far away from her would the ringing subside and his mind return to normalcy, but the remembrance of it clung to him like parasitic vines on a tree. Each day they grew larger and more ominous. He feared that one day they would strangle the very life from him. Until then, he would feast on the notion that he would die by being smothered alive.

Chapter 54

Back at the Conners Hill police station, Sgt. Alan Malloy was getting more than an earful from Chief Stanfield Grady.

"What I want to know," the chief shouted in Malloy's face, "is where you come off using the time and resources of this department to further your own ends? Don't you know your actions could jeopardize the credibility of the entire department, not to mention the town itself? "

Malloy winced but said nothing. Grady continued.

"As I understand it, you and two others picked up Vivian Blaine at Cee Edmunds' place and against her will took her to meet Vincent Sigman at some backwoods tobacco barn and that your intentions were totally honorable? Is that right?"

"That's right, chief," Malloy replied.

"And all you did to get her there was to tell her where you were going?"

"Not exactly," said Malloy.

"Well, what exactly?" the chief shouted.

"We told her we were taking her home but that we just had to make a short detour that we thought she would appreciate."

"Who the hell appreciates being kidnapped, Malloy? Tell me that. It would be easier to tell me that a woman who hasn't seen her family for nearly a week would ask you to stop for a hamburger and some fries on the way home. From all I know of her, Vivian Blaine is a normal human being, and normal human beings don't ask to be kidnapped just for the fun of it. Can't you come up with something a little more convincing than that?"

"Chief, it's like this. I know Vivian better than you do, and I know what kind of a woman she is. She likes a little adventure occasionally and she really isn't all that interested in her husband, anyway."

"You know this for a fact?" asked Grady.

"Well, I know that no woman who loves her husband would do the things she does with other men. It just isn't normal."

"And you know this from personal experience?"

"As personal as I'd care to discuss, but from what I've seen and heard, in my opinion she's a nymphomaniac."

"So you believe she has a severe psychological problem?"

"Yeah, I guess you could call it that."

"Then when you took her to see these men, you knew that it might be for some reason other than just talking?"

"Not really. I knew that Sigman just wanted to talk to her. At least, that's what he told me. I don't think he had any thing going with her. He just wanted to talk business with her."

"What kind of business?"

"The casino business. He wanted to know if Vivian would help him convince some local businessmen to change their mind."

"And did Sigman pay you to be his errand boy?"

"What do you think I am, Chief, a pimp?"

"We've already established that, haven't we, Malloy?"

"The question is: what are you getting out of it? What's the deal? And don't tell me there's nothing in it for you. You may know Vivian Blaine better than I do, but I know you better than you know yourself. You don't do anything unless there's something in it for you, right?"

"Well, maybe so, Chief. After all, it's a dog-eat-dog world. We've all got to look out for number one."

"That may be the way you see it, Malloy, but it isn't what I see. The police in this town are sworn public servants. Our job is to help look out for people who can't look out for themselves, or at least to see that all those who are looking out for number one aren't trampling on the rights of those who happen to be somewhere down the line."

"I thought I would be helping bring a new source of revenue to town that would ultimately benefit all the town residents," Malloy pleaded.

"Come on, Malloy. Just when did you get to be so public spirited? I know there's more to it than that. Just tell me what it is that Sigman promised you if this casino business deal goes through and our little discussion will be over."

"Well, Chief, he did say that I might become one of his floor managers once a casino is built in Conners Hill. It would mean better hours and twice the pay I get as a policeman. I could probably make more money than a small town police chief. I mean who would turn down an offer like that?"

"Okay, Sergeant, I get the picture, but I've got one for you, too. As of now you are free to look for a better paying job anywhere you like, because you no longer have one here. I'll give you three weeks severance pay and that's it."

"Chief, you can't be serious."

"Watch me," Grady replied.

Chapter 55

Things had not gone much better for Vivian once Malloy dropped her off at her home. Ernie met her at the front door and lashed out at her as soon as she was inside the house.

"Where have you been for the past week, Viv? We've all been worried sick about you? Why didn't you call us or let us know what was going on?"

"I'm sorry, Ernie, but I was knocked out and unconscious for a while. When I came to I didn't know where I was or who had revived me. I had gotten a head injury and it took a while to get oriented and clear as to what happened. By then I discovered that the person who had taken me in didn't have a car or a phone and had no way to contact you or the police."

"How the hell do you expect me to believe that, Viv? Who in today's world doesn't have a car or a phone, or at least access to one or the other? The fact is I can't believe anything you say to me any more. I told you before that I'd taken about all I could take from you, and this is the last straw. I want you out of this house as soon as you can pack your bags. I want you to forget that you ever knew me or that you have two children who love and adore you. As far as I'm concerned, they no longer have a mother, and I no longer have a wife, if I ever had one."

"Ernie, I understand how you feel. I can't blame you for what you feel. I'd feel the same way if I had been in your shoes. But you've got to understand that what has happened had nothing to do with you or me. I've learned my lesson this past week. I know now why I've treated you so badly and why I've treated a lot of other people badly as well. Psychologically, I have been a major disaster. I never intended it to be that way, it just was. I'm terribly ashamed of myself and of what I've put you and our family through, but, believe me, I'm sure it's all behind me now."

"It may be behind you, Vivian, but it's not behind me. I will have to live every day of the rest of my life with the memory that you betrayed not only me and my family but your own children. I will go to my grave with the stigma of having lived nearly a decade of my life with an unfaithful wife. Do you know how that makes me look—like an idiot and a fool, that's how. I've had a hard enough time looking my friends and family in the eye for the past five years. I don't think I can face them any longer unless I sever our relationship and move on. I've already made inquiries about a new job in the western part of the state, and I've contacted a Realtor to put this house on the market as soon as possible. The sooner you can get your things together and move out, the better for all of us."

"Is there no other way we can get past this, Ernie? I really am a changed woman. I know I've been a terrible burden to you for a long time, but for the first time I can see my way out of a long, dark tunnel. I don't know if I can make it into the light without you and the kids."

'Vivian, you dug the hole you're in and you let your ambition or your obsession keep pulling you deeper and deeper, and unfortunately you pulled a lot of other people in with you. I can forget what you did to yourself, but I can't forget what you've done to the rest of us. It's a tragedy we'll never outlive. So, Vivian, do us all a favor and leave us now. Let all of us get on with our lives and forget the past. As far as I'm concerned, the past is already nothing more than a memory trace."

Tears began to flow from Vivian's eyes. She was truly sorry for what she had done. She wished she could turn back the clock and change the past, but she knew it was not possible. What was done was done. She would have to resolve to do the best she could and move on. It would be difficult, but she had faced difficulties before. As far as she knew, she still had a job in Wolf Johnson's office, and she still carried some favor with Lawrence Cameron and a number of other business people in Conners Hill. She believed she could keep working and she would manage. It wasn't the end of the world.

Chapter 56

At the Conners Hill Police Station, Jesse Stallings and Dave Devlin were thanking Chief Stanfield Grady for having his men pick up Vivian and return her home. Grady was a little surprised that they had come to the station to thank him personally.

"All I did was have her picked up and taken home," Grady said. "You were the ones who let me know where she was. We just got her back to Ernie's today and we haven't tried to question her as to what happened or how she came to be at Cee Edmunds' place. No doubt there's more to the story than meets the eye at this point. I'm sure you two know more than I do, seeing as how Stallings here is the one who let me know where she was. We won't have any idea whether there will be any charges against anyone until we have a chance to talk to Vivian and find out exactly what happened.. When a woman gets the kind of treatment I understand she got, there's not much doubt someone is guilty of assault and battery if not attempted murder. If that's the case, we want to know who did it and what their motive was."

"I don't think Dave and I are going to be able to help you out on that one, Stan, although we do have some suspicions. But neither of us believes Cee had anything to do with Vivian's injuries. After all, he was the one who let us know that she was at his cabin. If he had assaulted her in any way, I doubt he would have let us know she was there."

"Well, you never know," said Grady. "Stranger things have happened. The good Lord has a way of allowing us to create some pretty unbelievable things sometimes. Perhaps we see it more often than the general public because we get called in to help clean up the mess. You know what I'm talking about, Jesse. You've had to report on what has happened perhaps more often than you would have liked. And Dave, here has no doubt been called in on cases that he would probably not have wanted to handle. Life doesn't hand us what we want all the time, but sometimes it does hand us what we need. I doubt that Vivian needed the trouble she found, but there's no doubt in my mind that she chose it for herself. She's a beautiful and intelligent woman but as complicated as she is well put together....I've heard too many stories about some of her shenanigans to know she's not entirely blameless in whatever complications there are. But so much for Vivian, what else have you guys been up to that I should know about.

"Well, Chief, now that you mention it, we're a little bit interested in what's going on with regard to Sam Slocum and his campaign to promote casino gambling. Sam seems to be a nice guy for the most part, but he's ambitious and I suspect a little devious," said Jesse. "Janice and I attended one of his dinner parties a week or so ago and Sam let us know in no uncertain terms that he intends to pursue this idea until it becomes a reality."

Stanfield Grady looked a bit perplexed. "Jesse, whatever you know about Sam's business is more than I know. I don't get invited to dinner parties by the town's upper crust very often, unless it's a benefit to raise money for some charity or a party big enough to warrant crowd control or some other police protection. Then they invite me to be polite and make sure we've provided the services they wanted. Of course, I've known Sam a long time. I don't think he's a bad guy despite having a few rough spots in his business dealings. I've never known him to do anything criminal or even dishonest, unless you include counting the cards in a friendly poker game, and that's not against the law."

"Have you ever known Sam to deal with anyone who might not have the same reputation, Stan, somebody with connections outside of Conners Hill?" asked Devlin.

"Not that I know of, Dave. Of course, there is this guy Vince something who's been in town for several weeks. I hear he's from somewhere up North and that he and Sam have been hanging around together. All I know about him is that he's a developer or investor of some kind. As he hasn't gotten into any trouble, I've had no reason to do a background check on him."

Devlin wasn't surprised but he was a little amused. "Would it surprise you, Chief, to know that this Vince Sigman's given name is Vincent Sigmanelli and that some of his building projects up north have been underwritten by investment houses with ties to the New York mafia?"

"Yeah, that would surprise me and disturb me as well, Devlin. I want to know anything that happens in this town that could cause me or anyone else trouble. Besides, it makes me wonder a little bit about a couple of my men."

"Why is that, Chief.?"

"Well, the fact is I fired one of them just this afternoon. Told him to turn in his badge and equipment and not come back."

"That wouldn't be Alan Malloy, would it, Chief?"

"Yeah, Devlin, how did you know?"

"I didn't, but I do know a little about Malloy, and I know that he's been invited to several of these high-highfalutin' parties at Sam Slocum's house, or he's been to several of them at least."

"How would you know that?"

"Well, I'm not at liberty to give you all the details, Chief, but the fact is I found out while I was doing a routine surveillance for a client. I followed Malloy and a couple of your officers to a house in Bramblegate once, and while I was there I saw Malloy and the other two go into Sam's. I also observed a number of attorneys and a judge as they arrived at the house, as well a car load of young women, a car, which incidentally, included one Vivian Blaine."

"Jesus, Devlin. Why didn't you tell me about any of this?"

"At the time, I didn't think anything about it, I didn't even know whose house it was until I talked to Jesse here, and I didn't have any reason to suspect that anything criminal or underhanded was going on. I just thought it strange that a couple of Conners Hill cops would be socializing in plain clothes with some of the town's upper crust."

"I would like to have known that sooner," the chief replied. "It would have made my job a lot easier when I decided to fire Malloy."

"Why's that, Chief?"

"Because when I sent Alan out to pick up Vivian this morning, he took a couple of other guys with him, and after he picked her up at Edmunds' place, he didn't take her straight home. He took her out to an abandoned tobacco barn to meet with you-know-who."

"Who you know who?"

"The guy you call Vincent Simanelli."

"Chief, there's just one little thing that bothers me here," said Dave Devlin.

"Yeah, what's that?"

"The night I followed Malloy to Slocum's house, he had come to the police station from a local tavern. He and the other two guys left the station to go to Sam's and I had watched as all three of them arrived at the station. They were all wearing their uniforms when they went in, but they had on civilian coats and ties when they came out. I also heard the bartender at the tavern tell Malloy that you had called them back to the station and that you had an assignment for them, presumably at Sam's house. If that's the case, why wouldn't you have known about Malloy being at Sam's?"

"Oh, I knew about Malloy going to Slocum's house all right. Sam had called me at home after dinner that night and told me he had Judge Feldman and several lawyers from Selwin coming over to his house and he wanted to make sure they would know some of the people there. I knew Alan and the other two patrolmen had appeared in Feldman's court a number of times and that they were on good terms. Feldman thought Alan was a good cop and could be trusted. On the other hand, I thought so, too, but there you go. Life hands you those unexpected surprises occasionally, and this was one of them?"

"It sure does, Chief. Vivian Blaine and this whole setup is something I would never have expected to run into in a small town like Conners Hill."

Jesse Stallings had listened to the entire conversation between Chief Grady and Devlin with interest and some slight amusement. His only thought was that business and intrigue went together like bread and butter. In fact, he thought, intrigue was the butter that sometimes made the business bread so enticing.

Chapter 57

A week later Vivian Blaine had moved out of the house in the Timberwood Forest subdivision and into a small apartment in a complex near downtown Conners Hill. She already missed her two children and she missed Ernie more than she thought possible, but she had made up her mind to ride out the separation and an impending divorce and get on with her life. It was going to be more difficult than she had anticipated, for when she returned to work at Wolf Johnson's office, she was received less warmly than she expected. At the end of the week, Johnson informed her that she would no longer be needed at the firm.

"I really regret this, Vivian," Johnson explained, "but I'm afraid that too many rumors about your extra-curricular activities and your breakup with Ernie have become a serious liability. After all, we have a reputation to maintain, and anything that brings even the slightest hint of impropriety by anyone working here affects the public perception as to who we are and what we do. It's a terrible shame because you are an exceptionally talented woman and you've done a fine job for us. But business is business and we operate in an unforgiving environment."

Johnson informed Vivian that he would provide her with a month's severance pay and that he would be willing to help her find another job somewhere else. "I'm afraid that for your own sake, it would be better for you to go to work somewhere other than in Conners Hill. I'm sure you understand that."

"Of course," Vivian replied. It's okay to ride the donkey when the wind is coming from the right direction, but when it changes, it's time to get off and leave the animal behind. All women are still animals to be used and abused, she thought.

Once she had cleaned out her desk and said her good-byes, Vivian never looked back. She would indeed leave Conners Hill, but not before taking care of the business she had decided was her purpose in life. She would leave town, but she would leave her mark on it for others to observe and judge.

That afternoon she called Vincent Sigman at the motel where he was staying. She arranged to meet him that evening for dinner and to discuss the details of the effort to persuade some of the local opponents of casino gambling to change their minds on the matter. Sigman said he would pick her up at her apartment.

"Aren't you worried that being seen with me might jeopardize your standing among the better class of people in this town?" she asked.

"I don't know any of the better class of people in this town outside of you and Sam and Lawrence," he replied.

"Gee, Vince, you sure know how to cheer a girl up! I'll be waiting at eight."

After picking Vivian up, Sigman drove her to a large but almost secluded restaurant on the outskirts of Selwin called Staley's. It was quiet and dimly lit, a nearly perfect setting for a romantic evening. The red-jacketed waiters were extremely attentive and each course of the meal was served with the flair of a theatrical production.

"You come to this place often?" Vivian asked Vincent.

"Only when I want to impress someone," he replied.

"Do you think I need being impressed?"

"Actually, I'm trying to impress the waiters," Vincent grinned.

"How's that?"

"It's not often they get to wait on a woman as beautiful as you," said Vincent. "In their eyes I must either be one of the handsomest, richest or smartest guys in the world, or else I'm the luckiest."

"Vincent, whatever you are, you are full of it."

"Absolutely," Sigman replied.

Oh, my God, thought Vivian, he sounds just like Cee.

After a dinner of char-broiled steaks, red wine and pleasant conversation, Vincent outlined his plan for Vivian's ascension to the position of Queen Bee of Conners Hill.

"First of all," he said, "you will need to provide me with all the audio and videotape you have of yourself and the people we are interested in persuading that casinos are in their best interest. As far as you are concerned personally, that will be the end of it. We will take care of the rest."

"But Vincent, if I am in these tapes, how can I be kept out of it. My face and pretty much the rest of me will be recognized. I'll be the laughing stock of Conners Hill, not the Queen Bee."

"Oh, but you won't," Vincent replied. "Your face will be blurred and your voice altered. All that will be recognizable to whoever might access these things will be an unknown female and the men with her. They might as well be dallying with a hooker from New York. They will be recognizable to anyone in Conners Hill, but your image will be an unknown entity. We can change your hair color and erase any identifying body marks you might have."

"But won't it be evident that these images have been altered? I mean, after all, law enforcement people today have access to the same kinds of electronic equipment you or your people have. Isn't there a way that they can backtrack and find out who I am?"

"Not really, as long as we have disposed of the original tapes. Besides, they will have a difficult if not impossible job of determining where these recordings came from. I'm not going to go into the details of it, but we would put the information on a web site which would take a very long and complicated process to track down. By then, our casinos will be up and running"

"Why would you put them on a web site? Wouldn't that make them accessible to anyone?"

"Not necessarily. Access to the web sites can be encrypted and locked and made as impenetrable as a bank's accounts. That part of it won't be hard to do, but it will make it virtually impossible for anyone to see except the people you want to see it."

"And who would that be?"

" Just you and the men who are with you on the recordings."

"So what difference will it make if we're the only ones with access to them?"

"Well, there will be one other group of people who might be able to see or hear the recordings, but only if the men involved don't listen to our advice."

"Who would they be?"

"The wives."

"And I will have access to the web site?"

"Of course."

"And will I be able to determine who gets access?"

"Well, that would be a little dangerous perhaps, but, yes, I think you should be able to make that determination."

"Then I'll do it. I'll get you the tapes as soon as possible."

"Good, then we can get on with the program."

Unbeknown to Vivian, Vincent Sigman already had all the tapes he needed. Lawrence Cameron had turned what he had over to Sam Slocum, who had turned them over to him. The trio merely wanted to include Vivian in their scheme in order to have a scapegoat if anything went wrong and the authorities were indeed able to trace the tapes back to their source. If so, they would argue that Vivian was the instigator of the blackmail attempt and that it had nothing to do with their casino plans because the plans included one final element. It was just one more little detail that Vincent had not explained to Vivian, but it was critical to their safety. They had decided that Vivian should be the one to inform the local businessmen or their wives that the tapes existed.

Chapter 58

Vivian dropped in on Lawrence Cameron the next day. She told Cameron she wanted him to turn over all the tapes to Vincent so that he could have the web site set up. Once done, they could be viewed by the wives whose husbands' failed to support the casino business. There were seven men in all, but four of them made up a majority on the Conners Hill Town Council. Sam Slocum felt it was imperative that the council pass a resolution supporting the casino business before presenting it to the legislature. He also needed the Council's support in order to build the state's first casino in Conners Hill. Having its location in the center of one of North Carolina's major metropolitan districts would give it proximity to more than a million people within a 100-mile radius, as well as access to the media outlets of three of the state's largest cities. Positive media exposure through newspapers and television was critical to the success of the project. That was one of the reasons he wanted Jesse Stallings and at least two of the daily newspapers' editors in his corner.

Vincent Sigman had reported to Slocum that Vivian could be counted on to apply pressure to a good many of the errant businessmen who had enjoyed the pleasure of her company more than once. Sigman said it would not constitute blackmail on her part because she would be asking nothing for herself, but simply that the businessmen would give "due consideration" to the proposals of Sam and his associates. As an incentive, she would explain that she was putting together an Internet web site that would be accessible only to the wives of the gentlemen concerned. She would tell neither the businessmen nor their wives the contents of the web site, only that their wives might find it extremely interesting. The web site would be hosted by a private Internet service provider in New Jersey and would not be accessible to law enforcement authorities in North Carolina, nor would it be of interest to New Jersey authorities as it would contain information relating only to individuals living in North Carolina who had no ties to business or government in New Jersey. The New Jersey ISP would merely provide access to a computer server owned by a multi-tiered corporation in New York. Moreover the site would contain only information about those individuals and an unnamed female companion. Vivian would have no connection to the Internet site nor the corporation. She would merely have provided the video tapes on the site to a New Jersey address provided by Sigman.

Perfect Imperfection

Two days later Vincent called Vivian to tell her the web site was ready to go on-line and that she should begin preparing to inform seven wayward husbands of the importance of their positive vote for the project. Vivian thought it odd that Vincent had been able to get the web site on-line so fast, but she assumed it was because his associates were very good at such things. Two more days passed and Vivian was able to tell Vincent that she had contacted all the town council members and that they were ready for a vote. In the meantime she checked out the web site herself, the address of which, waywardhusbands .com, was unmistakable to those searching for it. Vivian wanted to see if the passwords admitting Internet users to the individual tapes were working. As soon as she was satisfied everything was in order, she sent a package of notes in envelopes to a friend in California to be mailed from a common drop box. The notes were to be mailed to specific wives only if the friend received instructions from Vivian to mail them. If a husband did not support the casino business, the note with the name of the web site and the password for his individual tape would be mailed to the wife.

The note, addressed and written in a computer-generated script, contained the following message:

Dear Mrs. _____

This is to inform you that your husband has become involved in a compromising personal situation. If you should choose to know the extent of his extracurricular activities, enter the following password into the web site whose address is waywardhusbands.com.

The password for each recording contained ten letters and numbers generated randomly by computer. There was no return address.

Vincent called Vivian to find out if she had indeed contacted each of the council members. When she said she did, he asked, "Did you run into any major opposition?"

"Not at all," said Vivian.

"And are satisfied that all the councilmen will do the right thing?"

"Absolutely," Vivian said.

""Good, then we're on our way to Raleigh as soon as the Council has met and voted."

A week later at a Conners Hill Council meeting, Mayor Robert Ziglar introduced the resolution proposed by the Conners Hill Chamber of Commerce to recommend that the state legislature take up a proposal to allow casino gambling in North Carolina. After speeches both pro and con from fifteen or more residents, including Sam Slocum, Lawrence Cameron and Alan Malloy, Ziglar called for a vote of the council members.

"All those in favor of this proposal, please raise your hands," said Ziglar.

No hands went up.

"All those opposed to this proposal, please raise your hands," the mayor continued.

All seven council members raised their hands.

The mayor banged his gavel on the table. "The ayes have it," he said. "The matter is closed."

Slocum, Cameron and Malloy, along with many Chamber members, sat for a moment with stunned looks on their faces. Afterward they rose from their seats and made their way back toward the Council Chamber exit. Vincent Sigman was standing near the door. He, too, was as perplexed as the others.

As Slocum brushed past Sigman, he glared at the New Yorker in anger.

"What the hell happened here, Vincent? You gave me your word that it was in the bag."

"Vivian told me she had contacted everybody concerned," said Sigman. "I believed her."

"Then you had better not take much stock in what you believe."

When he reached the motel where he was staying, Sigman called Vivian at her apartment. No one answered. A voice recording said the telephone had been disconnected. Vincent went to his car and drove to her apartment building. He knocked repeatedly on her door,. No one answered. He went to the next apartment and knocked. A woman came to the door.

"Pardon me, but I was looking for your neighbor Vivian Blaine," said Vincent.

"Oh, she's not there," the woman replied.

"I know that, but can you tell me where she might be."

"She moved out early this morning. She didn't say where she was going. She merely said she needed a vacation and would be gone for some time. What did you say your name was?"

"Sigman, Vincent Sigman."

"Oh, Mr. Sigman, Vivian left a message for you She said you would understand. Wait here a moment and I'll get it for you." She returned shortly with a sealed envelope in her hand.

"Here it is. I hope it isn't bad news or anything. It isn't like Vivian to be the bearer of bad news. I liked her a lot."

"I'm sorry, I didn't get your name," said Vincent.

"Bebe Bullis," the woman said.

Vincent waited until he was back in his car to open the note. "Dear Vincent," it said. "I think I have made a terrible mistake. I had an unsigned Microsoft Word message mailed from Miami to each of the council members saying they should not vote to turn down the casino proposal or else their wives might come across some very unsavory information about them. Unfortunately, I failed to review the text of the message before sending them to a friend in Florida to mail. When I went back and read it on my computer, I discovered that instead of saying 'You should not vote to turn down the casino proposal,' I accidentally dropped the 'not' from the note. I mistakenly said they should vote to turn down the proposal. Perhaps it was a Freudian slip. I hardly ever tell anyone not to do something that would make them happy. Sam said I should make the note positive. I guess I did. Love, Vivian."

Vincent smiled a knowing smile, then he bit his lip until it bled. It didn't hurt near as much as the fact that Vivian had included him among the men she felt she should betray. Two days later he would return to New York not only empty-handed but minus the one hundred thousand dollars he had advanced to Sam to get the casino project underway. He had learned a hard lesson, but he had learned it well. He would never trust another beautiful woman again.

Chapter 59

At the Conners Hill News, Jesse Stallings sat at his desk putting the finishing touches on an editorial he hoped would touch the heart of the community. It was an editorial that began with a tribute to the Conners Hill Town Council for having turned down the proposal to support casino gambling in the town and the state and for having had the courage to do so in the face of what seemed to be strong support from a majority of members of the local Chamber of Commerce. Although the Chamber's executive director had been against the proposal from the beginning, the membership had been swayed by the argument that a casino in Conners Hill would attract more people to town, as well as more business, and that anything that was good for business was good for the people of the town. As the director was hired by the membership to do their bidding, he had no choice but to present their wishes to the town council.

Stallings applauded not only the council members who voted to defeat the measure but also Mayor Robert Ziglar and those who, like Greg Irwin and Kingston Armour, had worked behind the scenes to oppose the project. The three had weathered a barrage of pro-growth, pro-business propaganda and knew that their own businesses might suffer some adverse effects from their actions. Nevertheless, they stuck to their belief that what was truly good for a community was what was good for the people of the community as a whole, not just for those who would profit immediately and directly from an action they considered to be unwise in the long run.

Lastly, Stallings concluded the editorial by saying there were certain individuals whose strength and courage under the most adverse conditions of all, those of an assault on their behavior, their character and even their very lives, had led them to help defeat the casino project in ways that most of the community would never know, or, if known, could not possibly understand.

Jesse was not able to say that Vivian Blaine, who was generally regarded as a wayward wife and a despicable and wanton woman had, in an act of moral courage, turned the tide of personal hypocrisy and backroom political treachery into a mere whimper of power. He merely noted that there were some people who had lost not only their reputations and their livelihood by opposing the casinos, but had lost the one thing which all men and women cherished most dearly, their spouses and their children.

Those women in the community who knew what had happened would know to whom Stallings referred. And while they would not talk openly about it, they would sometimes talk admiringly among themselves of the woman who had not only saved their town but who had saved them from the embarrassment of having to expose their own families. They did not mention Vivian by name, but they felt that in some way her association with their husbands, though painful to the core, had turned out well in the end. Most of them concluded that Vivian's imperfect behavior had led to a perfect means of keeping their husbands in line in the future.

Finally, Stallings concluded the editorial by saying that one member of the community who had been frequently seen as an immensely flawed individual and who was looked upon by most of the townspeople as an oddball and hopeless eccentric had in fact been the catalyst for what had occurred. "Unfortunately, such is human nature that this individual will no doubt go on being a rebel and an outcast scorned and ridiculed by those who judge others simply by the way they look, speak or dress. Such judgments are often the result of those things we fear are a part of ourselves, and until we can accept ourselves with our flaws and our shortcomings, we cannot possibly accept those who present us with a reflection of ourselves."

Chapter 60

Ten years later

A philosopher once said that "time exists only to provide a means of measuring the fact that things change." In ten years Conners Hill had changed from a fast-growing town of 20,000 people to a bustling city of 40,000. Most everything that people cared about had changed, including the people themselves. They realized it only on the faces and in the lives of other people.

Jesse Stallings, for one, had reached his sixties and retired from the Conners Hill News in order to pursue his lifelong ambition to write novels. Calling most of his work "white lies," he said he had been influenced in part by the novelist John O'Hara, who once noted that he had quit the newspaper business and begun writing fiction in order to "tell the truth."

Like Stallings, Dave Devlin had become a novelist and had turned out a string of colorful mysteries featuring a private investigator named Harry Paine and his sidekick,

Mona Morgan. The stories were so successful that Devlin was often hired to speak to audiences both about writing and about the life of a private detective.

Not everyone Stallings had known over the years was as fortunate. In his early seventies, Mayor Robert Ziglar, who had led the conservative political movement in Conners Hill through most of the last half of the twentieth century, had come down with Parkinson's Disease and was a mere shell of his former self. Nonetheless, he had left behind a coterie of political admirers who sought to continue his dream of turning the small town into an icon of economic growth and progress.

The years had done some damage to others in Conners Hill, some of it irreparable and some not so drastic. The defeat of the state casino referendum was a bitter blow to Sam Slocum and Alan Malloy, but they weathered the storm. Both men moved away from the town to other states and other enterprises. The last time anyone heard from Slocum, he had formed a development company and opened a new gambling casino near Gulfport, Mississippi, replacing one that had been ripped apart by a hurricane which had also decimated a large part of New Orleans. He was being backed by some unnamed investors from New York. While Sam was working to put his project together, his wife, Judith, had taken over as the chef of an elegant restaurant on the outskirts of Gulfport and was becoming well-known for her culinary innovations.

Lawrence Cameron was the pro-casino businessman least affected by the defeat of the project in Conners Hill. Cameron had helped in the attempt to force a favorable vote on the issue, but as far as most people knew, he had no involvement at all. Thus when the effort failed, Cameron went back to doing what he normally did, which was to keep his business and politics separate. Within five years, he found his trucking business in a decline and he moved on to partial ownership in a beer and wine distributorship. He moved to another town in North Carolina and continued to prosper. He also continued to hire at least one secretary based not on her professional abilities but on her stunning good looks.

Vincent Sigman's fortunes diminished somewhat after the Conners Hill casino debacle, especially among higher ranking members of his family and their associates. However, Sigman used his expertise, his personal charm and his own money to recover and continue his usually successful development projects.

Vivian Blaine had lost her family and her reputation in the ten years she spent in Conners Hill, but she had not lost her moral fiber nor her ability to recover from what appeared to be a total personal disaster. Five years after leaving town, she had turned up as the owner-operator of a highly successful video business called Vivian's Videos in Myrtle Beach, South Carolina. She charged $250 for a two-hour video and hired college students on summer break to follow families around with small, hand-held cameras to record their activities. She paid the students $75 for a day's work . She corresponded frequently with Bebe Bullis and Nancy Seemore, and she sent letters of thanks each year to Cee Edmunds and Jesse Stallings. At the change of season each year Vivian was visited by Ernie Blaine and their two children. They stayed with her for a week at her beach front house. At least once a year, when Ernie and the children were not there, Vincent Sigman flew into Myrtle Beach to visit her as well.

Sadly, five years after Vivian left town, Cee Edmunds was taking one of his late night walks down the center of Main Street when he was attacked and severely beaten by a street gang known as Los Angeles Diablos, or The Devil's Angels. They had heard that Cee was not only a strange and detestable figure but that he was a Zen Buddhist as well. None of the Angels knew what a Zen Buddhist was, but they thought it was not a proper religion and was therefore anathema to any right-thinking person. A night-duty policeman discovered Cee's battered body and immediately called for an ambulance. He was taken to the new Conners Hill Hospital where he died on the operating table. Two days later a graveside service was held at the Mount Gur cemetery. The only people attending the service were Jesse Stallings, Dave Devlin and Vivian Blaine.

A final note: About seven years after the defeat of the state casino project, a woman named Beverly "Bev" Perdue was elected governor of North Carolina.

Printed in the United States
213108BV00001B/1/P